Sugar Apple Fairy Tale

The Silver Sugar Master and the Obsidian Fairy

1

Miri Mikawa
Illustration by Aki

NEW YORK

Sugar Apple Fairy Tale 1

Miri Mikawa

Translation by Nicole Wilder
Cover art by Aki

This book is a work of fiction. Names, characters, places, and incidents are the product of the author's imagination or are used fictitiously. Any resemblance to actual events, locales, or persons, living or dead, is coincidental.

Yen On
150 West 30th Street, 19th Floor
New York, NY 10001

Visit us at yenpress.com facebook.com/yenpress twitter.com/yenpress
yenpress.tumblr.com instagram.com/yenpress

First Yen On Edition: September 2022
Edited by Yen On Editorial: Shella Wu, Kurt Hassler
Designed by Yen Press Design: Wendy Chan

Library of Congress Cataloging-in-Publication Data
Names: Mikawa, Miri, author. | Aki, 1967– illustrator. | Wilder, Nicole, translator.
Title: Sugar apple fairy tale / Miri Mikawa ; illustration by Aki ; translation by Nicole Wilder.
Other titles: Shuga appuru feari teiru. English
Description: First Yen On edition. | New York, NY : Yen On, 2022. |
Contents: v. 1. The silver sugar master and the obsidian fairy —
Identifiers: LCCN 2022022460 | ISBN 9781975350000 (v. 1 ; trade paperback)
Subjects: CYAC: Fantasy. | Candy—Fiction. | Fairies—Fiction. |
Bodyguards—Fiction. | LCGFT: Fantasy fiction. | Light novels.
Classification: LCC PZ7.1.M5538 Su 2022 | DDC [Fic]—dc23
LC record available at https://lccn.loc.gov/2022022460

ISBNs: 978-1-9753-5000-0 (paperback)
978-1-9753-5001-7 (ebook)

1 3 5 7 9 10 8 6 4 2

LSC-C

Printed in the United States of America

CONTENTS

The Silver Sugar Master and the Obsidian Fairy

Sugar Apple Fairy Tale

Lovelorn Young Master
Jonas
Fairy
Mithril
Fairy
Cathy
...Then I'll make some candy for you! I am a budding candy crafter, you know!
Mysterious Man
Hugh

Warrior Fairy
Challe
Do you like silver sugar? Or do you hate it?
Silver Sugar Master in the Making
Anne
Sugar Apple Fairy Tale
The Silver Sugar Master and the Obsidian Fairy
Silver Sugar Master
Special artisans who craft sacred confections worthy of the royal household. Only someone who has won a royal medal at the Royal Candy Fair may claim the title.

What's the matter, Anne? You can't sleep?

It's all right. We all have those days.

Since you're awake, why don't you let Mama tell you a story? An old tale passed down in the Kingdom of Highland, a story about fairies.

That's right, fairies. They're people with delicate wings on their backs. We've seen them working for wealthy households, haven't we?

Here, let's get you wrapped up in your blanket. That's right, good girl. All right now, I'll start the story.

A long, long time ago, in the distant past, when humans didn't even know how to use fire, there was a fairy kingdom here. The kingdom was ruled by a fairy monarch, and all the fairies lived in peace.

The fairies called their kingdom Highland. It means *the land that stands at the very top*, ruling over every living thing. Back then, the fairies enslaved humans, who were neither intelligent nor powerful.

Yes, it's true.

Now humans keep fairies as servants, but in the old days, the opposite was true. The fairies controlled the humans.

Got it? I'm going to continue.

The fairies were peace-loving. They always sought out beauty and joy.

For hundreds of years, they lived quietly, without change.

But the humans were different. They changed, bit by bit.

The humans worked hard and learned how to use fire without the fairies noticing. They gained intelligence. Then at last, they became aware. They realized they didn't have to work for the fairies.

That was five hundred years ago.

The humans staged a rebellion and took over Highland. They made the fairies their servants.

Hmm? Yes, you're right.

The fairies of today are pitiful creatures. Some people say they are foolish beings who lost to humans because they lived lives of indolence. But I don't think that's true. There were fewer fairies than humans, and I think they simply lost in a contest of strength.

Why do I think that? Well, it's said that fairies were the ones who discovered how to refine silver sugar from sugar apples. Fairies were the first in the world to make sugar candy.

They couldn't have been fools if they created something so wonderful.

That's why candy crafters like us mustn't look down on fairies, even if we're the only ones who don't.

I think we ought to treat them as friends.

That goes for you, too, Anne. Anne? ...Oh my, you fell asleep. What a good girl you are, Anne. Good night.

Sleep well, smile a lot, and grow up to be a kind girl, as sweet as sugar candy.

Chapter 1

THE SCARECROW AND THE FAIRY

The sun rose over the horizon, and the morning rays shone brightly on Anne's soft, pale cheek.

Sitting atop her wagon, Anne gripped the reins of her horse. A cool breeze blew softly past the hem of her cotton dress. The lace on her hem, simple but clean, fluttered slightly.

Anne took a deep breath and looked up at the sky.

The previous night's rain had washed all the dust out of the air. The autumn sky was clear and blue.

Today, Anne was setting out on her journey. Still gripping the reins in both hands, she gazed ahead.

The road was muddy, with deep ruts from the wheels of countless wagons.

Anne would be heading down that road alone. Her slender frame was taut with fear and anticipation.

But she felt a faint sense of hope in her heart as well.

Just then, a voice called out from behind her, "Anne!! Wait, Anne!"

Behind Anne's boxy, horse-drawn wagon was a cluster of simple stone houses that formed Knoxberry Village. This village in the northwest of the Kingdom of Highland had taken care of her for the past six months.

Ever since Anne was born, she had lived her life traveling from one place to another with her mother, Emma. Her time in Knoxberry Village was actually the longest she had ever spent in one place.

A tall, blond young man came running out of the village. He was

Jonas, the only son of the Anders family, which ran the confectionery in Knoxberry.

"Wah, I knew it!"

Anne ducked her head and whipped the horse. As the wagon started rolling, she turned back and waved.

"Jonas! Thanks, take care!"

"Wait, please. Anne, wait! Do you hate me?!"

"That's not why I'm leaving— Don't worry about that—," Anne answered loudly.

Catching his breath, Jonas shouted, "Well—well then, wait up!!"

"I've already made up my mind. Good-bye!"

The distance between them grew quickly. Jonas gradually slowed his pace and came to a stop. Still panting, he watched Anne in a daze.

Anne gave one last big wave, then turned forward again.

"Watch over me…Mama."

In early spring of that year, Anne's lively and cheerful mother, Emma, had fallen ill. They'd been passing through Knoxberry Village when it happened, and that was where they had stayed.

The people of the village were very kind to Anne and Emma, despite the fact that they were outsiders. They had offered to let the pair stay until Emma was well. Jonas and his family had lent a room free of charge to both mother and daughter during that time, perhaps out of camaraderie for fellow artisans.

However, Emma never recovered from her illness. She had passed away a few weeks prior.

"Find your own path in life and walk boldly down it, Anne. You can do anything. You're such a good girl, Anne. Don't cry."

Those were Emma's last words.

Then came the arrangements for the funeral and the formalities of a burial with the state church. While she was being hounded by such duties, Anne had let her sadness slide right off the surface of her heart. She'd grieved, but she hadn't been able to cry out loud.

Emma was now resting in a corner of the Knoxberry Village Cemetery. Thinking about it filled Anne's heart with a dismal feeling.

Half a month after her mother's death, Anne had finally finished all her various tasks and decided to begin her journey.

Three nights earlier, she'd informed the members of the Anders family, who had been taking care of her, that she was leaving.

"Anne, there's no way you can continue traveling on your own. Shouldn't you stay here with us in the village? And...you might...become my bride?" Jonas had whispered, grabbing Anne's hand after she'd announced her decision. He had pushed his soft, golden bangs out of his face, smiled, and looked at Anne with his sparkling eyes.

"I've always had feelings for you, Anne."

For half a year, Anne had been sleeping under the same roof as Jonas, but they'd never really had an intimate conversation. She never expected someone like him to propose to her.

Jonas was handsome, and his blue eyes were especially lovely. They were like the luxurious glass orbs imported from the kingdom in the south.

Even though Jonas was basically a stranger, she felt bewildered when he looked at her with those eyes.

Anne wasn't unhappy to have received his proposal. But she was determined to go.

She knew that Jonas might stop her if she went to say good-bye. That's why she had tried to leave the village stealthily, in the early morning. Even so, he must have noticed. Jonas had come after her.

"Marriage..." The word left her mouth absentmindedly. Anne felt the concept had absolutely nothing to do with her.

Jonas attracted a lot of attention from the girls who lived in the village.

Of course, one reason for his popularity was the fact that his family ran a prosperous confectionery shop.

Despite living in a provincial town like Knoxberry, Jonas was a descendant of the founder of the Radcliffe Workshop, one of the largest factions of candy crafters.

Anne had heard that there was a possibility he might be chosen as the Radcliffe Workshop's next maestro.

Before long, Jonas would probably be headed to the royal capital, Lewiston, for his training. That was the big rumor going around the village.

As the leader of a faction, if he was lucky, there was a possibility he could even become a Viscount.

To the daughters of a village in the countryside, Jonas must have seemed like a prince.

On the contrary, Anne was petite, despite being fifteen years old. She was skinny, with long arms and legs, and had fluffy hair the color of barley. Everywhere she went, she got teased for looking like a "scarecrow."

As far as her estate was concerned, she owned one old, boxy wagon and one worn-out horse.

The wealthy blond prince had proposed marriage to the poor little scarecrow. It was like some sort of dream.

"Well, whatever. There's no way that the prince is truly in love with a scarecrow like me," Anne mumbled with a bitter smile, then she whipped the horse.

Jonas had always been a playboy. He was especially sweet to all the girls. Anne was certain the only reason a boy like him would ever propose to a girl like her was that he felt sorry for her circumstances.

Anne didn't want to get married out of pity. The idea of marrying a prince and living happily ever after—like a princess in a fairy tale—didn't seem like much of a life goal.

Anne didn't hate Jonas. But the thought of living her life with him didn't appeal to her.

She wanted to stand on her own two feet and carve her own path in the world. That was the kind of life she wanted to lead.

Anne's father had been drafted to fight in a civil war not long after she was born, and he had died.

But Emma had raised Anne as a single mother and lived on.

She was able to do so because of her impressive skills as a Silver Sugar Master.

The Kingdom of Highland had many candy artisans, but Silver Sugar Masters, who were recognized by the crown as the best of the best, were rare.

Emma had become a Silver Sugar Master at the age of twenty.

Sweets made by ordinary candymakers couldn't compare with those made by Silver Sugar Masters, which fetched a much higher price. But in the villages and towns out in the countryside, expensive candies didn't sell very well.

In Lewiston, there was a much greater demand. However, famous Silver

Sugar Masters flocked to the royal capital, so it was difficult to compete with them and come out on top.

Thus, Emma had chosen to travel throughout the kingdom, seeking out customers who needed her sugar candy.

Strong-willed with boundless cheerfulness, Emma had always loved traveling.

Traveling was hard and dangerous, but she'd earned her own living and forged her own path. It was fun.

It would be so great if I became a Silver Sugar Master just like Mama.

Anne had always vaguely felt that way. So when Emma died and Anne had to decide how she would live the rest of her life, the deep love and respect she had for her mother had sprouted in Anne's heart as determination.

I will become a Silver Sugar Master.

But becoming a Silver Sugar Master was no ordinary feat. Anne knew that very well.

Every year in Lewiston, the royal family sponsors the Royal Candy Fair. In order to become a Silver Sugar Master, Anne would need to enter the fair and win the royal medal awarded to whoever earned first place.

Emma had entered the Royal Candy Fair when she was twenty and been awarded a royal medal. After that, she had been allowed to call herself a Silver Sugar Master.

Sugar candy is made using silver sugar refined from sugar apples. Such candy cannot be made from any other type of sugar. This is because no other sugar produces such beautiful results.

Silver sugar candies are used in all sorts of ceremonies, from weddings and funerals to coronations and coming-of-age celebrations.

It is even said that without the candy, no ceremony can begin.

Silver sugar invites joy and repels sorrow. Some say it holds the promise of sweet happiness, and it is considered a sacred food.

It is believed that in the age when Highland was still ruled by fairies, the fairies extended their life spans by consuming silver sugar candy.

Beautiful candy made with silver sugar contains a mysterious energy known as "essence."

Of course, humans cannot extend their life spans, not even by consuming silver sugar or sugar candies.

But they are able to take in some of that mysterious energy.

In fact, when humans consume beautiful sugar candy, unexpected good fortune often works its way into their lives, and they become luckier.

This is something humans came to understand after several hundred years.

It is also why monarchs stipulated strict qualifications for Silver Sugar Masters.

The royalty and nobility want the most sacred and alluring sugar candy to bestow upon themselves numerous blessings and great happiness. Even at the great autumn festival held to pray for the tranquility of the kingdom, the way the candy turns out may determine the fortunes of the country.

As always, the annual Royal Candy Fair would be held in Lewiston at the end of autumn.

Anne intended to participate and compete for the title of Silver Sugar Master, which was granted to only one person each year.

She had heard, now that Emma had passed away, there were twenty-three Silver Sugar Masters in the kingdom.

It was not a title that could be easily won.

But Anne was confident. After all, she hadn't spent fifteen years as an assistant to a Silver Sugar Master for nothing.

Anne's wagon rolled down the road, with fields of wheat stretching out to the left and right.

By the time the sun was high in the sky, she had arrived in Redington, the provincial capital and the largest town in the vicinity of Knoxberry.

Redington was a castle town, with streets radiating outward from a round central plaza. Up on a hill stood the castle from which the province of Redington was governed.

As Anne advanced slowly through the town on her wagon, she saw a crowd had formed in front of her and was blocking the street.

Anne shrugged and alighted from her wagon. She tapped lightly on the shoulder of a farmer who had his back to her.

"Hey, excuse me? What's everyone doing? The street is blocked, and I can't get my wagon through."

"Well…you can pass if you want, but are you brave enough to cut across that scene, young lady?"

"What scene?"

Anne peeked under the farmer's arm to see what everyone was staring at.

She spied a brawny man standing in a patch of mud, with a bow slung over his back and a sword hanging from his belt. He wore leather boots and a vest made of animal hides. He looked like a hunter.

"You little bastard!" the hunter shouted as he stomped again and again on a little lump on the ground. Mud splashed into the air. Each time the hunter's foot fell, the lump made a pitiful noise.

Looking carefully, Anne could see that the mound in the mud had the shape of a person, though palm-sized. On the back of the tiny individual lying facedown in the mud was a single dainty, translucent wing that was somehow unsoiled by the muck.

"Is that a fairy?! How cruel!" Anne cried quietly, and the farmer nodded.

Fairies are humanoid creatures who dwell in forests and meadows. They vary greatly in shape and size, but a distinctive characteristic shared by all are the two translucent wings on their backs.

Fairies have special abilities, and they can do all sorts of jobs well.

Anne had heard that royalty, nobles, and knights employed many fairies for different purposes.

Even common, middle-class households might have one or two to help with the housework.

In Jonas's house, there was a fairy named Cathy who was about the size of a palm as well. She looked after Jonas's daily needs and helped with the preparation of sugar candy.

"It's one of the fairy hunter's worker fairies. Looks like it tried to take its wing back and escape." The farmer lowered his voice and pointed stealthily toward the hunter.

In the fairy hunter's hand was a single thin wing. It matched the one on the back of the fairy in the mud.

In order to control fairies, slavers tear off one wing and keep it.

A fairy's wings are the source of their life force. A fairy can live with one wing separated from their body, but if that wing is damaged, the fairy weakens and dies. To compare it to human physiology, the wings are like the fairy's heart. Any human would tremble in fear if someone else held their heart captive. No one can disobey the person gripping their heart.

So by stealing one of their wings, slavers can make their fairies follow their commands.

But fairies don't want to be slaves. Many of them try to take back their wings and escape without their masters' knowledge.

"Even for a fairy, that's pretty cruel treatment."

"That fairy is gonna die!"

The people in the crowd murmured to one another, but no one moved.

Anne looked up at the farmer beside her and the other men around her.

"Hey, everyone! Are you going to let him get away with such heartless behavior?!"

But the people around Anne averted their eyes, seemingly fearful.

The farmer mumbled weakly, "I feel bad for the poor thing, but that fairy hunter has a violent temper. I'm afraid he'll retaliate… Besides, it's only a fairy…"

"What do you mean, 'only a fairy'?! If we hesitate, he's going to die! Fine, I'll go!"

Anne pushed past the farmer and stepped forward.

"Hey, a young girl like you shouldn't go out there!"

"I am not a child. I'm fifteen. In this country, girls are considered adults at age fifteen, right? So I'm legally an adult. I would be ashamed of myself for the rest of my life if, as a full-grown adult, I stood by and watched a fairy get tortured to death. This is no joke."

Anne drew herself to her full height and walked quickly toward the fairy hunter.

Perhaps because he was so agitated, the hunter didn't notice Anne. Trampling the fairy under the sole of his boot, he gripped the wing in his hands.

"Let me show you what I'm gonna do to your wing!"

"Stop it, you insolent dolt! Stop it!!"

The fairy bravely flailed his little arms and legs, kicking up mud. He shrieked in a shrill, piercing voice.

However, the fairy hunter mercilessly squeezed the wing between his fingers.

Down in the mud, the fairy let out another scream.

"You filthy thievin' fairy, I'll kill ya!"

The hunter pulled harder, as if to tear the wing in half. That was the moment Anne stepped up behind him. She bent her knees and charged forward.

"Oh, excuse me!!"

The hem of Anne's dress flew up as she shouted. With one foot, she delivered a powerful kick to the back of the fairy hunter's knee. It was Anne's signature move, her knockout blow—the knee buckler.

The fairy hunter was caught off guard, and his knee gave way immediately. He lost his balance. His mouth was still open in surprise when he fell face-first into the muddy street.

In the same instant that the curious onlookers burst into laughter, the fairy, suddenly released from under the man's boot, sprang up nimbly. Anne hopped over the man's head and quickly grabbed the fairy's wing from his enslaver's hand.

"Why, you!!" the hunter shouted, lifting his muddy face.

Anne effortlessly jumped out of his way. She extended the recovered wing to the fairy, who was standing there looking dazed.

"Here. This is yours, right?"

The fairy seemed startled, but he quickly snatched his wing back. His face was covered in mud, and only his blue eyes sparkled with a strange light.

The fairy looked up at Anne and shouted, "Tch! Don't expect me to say thanks to a human!!"

Holding his wing tightly in his arms, he dashed past the feet of the onlookers, who gasped and made room for him to pass. The fairy cast a backward glance at the astonished crowd, then disappeared toward the outskirts of town like a swift wind.

Anne shrugged. "Oh well, I am one of those awful humans, I suppose."

Dripping muddy water from his chin, the fairy hunter stood up and started shouting, "How're you gonna repay me, little girl?! You just let my valuable worker fairy escape!!"

Anne turned to him and said, "But, mister, you were going to kill that fairy, weren't you? So what does it matter as long as he's gone?"

"What'd you say?!"

The enraged fairy hunter raised his arm.

But the crowd surrounding them immediately voiced their collective outrage.

"You're an adult—are you going to raise your hand against a child?!"

"That girl is right!"

"You're acting barbaric!!"

The man flinched under the harsh criticism of the crowd. Anne looked the man directly in the eye, without fear.

The fairy hunter let out a small groan and lowered his hand.

"Thank you," Anne said sarcastically. "I'm glad you're such a kind person. And since you're so kind, I know that you're going to treat fairies nicely from now on, too. How wonderful!" She smiled at him sweetly.

The fairy hunter's expression was inscrutable, neither angry nor smiling.

"Bye, then!" Anne said a simple farewell to the fairy hunter, passed through the crowd that was praising her enthusiastically, and returned to her horse and wagon. "That makes me so mad. People are so cruel. Treating fairies badly just because they're fairies!" Anne mumbled angrily.

Fairies are built a little differently from humans. But they have thoughts and feelings, and even speak human languages.

Anne didn't think of them as being any different. Her conscience ached at the idea of using fairies as slaves.

That was why Emma had never employed a fairy.

We don't use fairies.

That had been Emma and Anne's belief. And yet—

Anne's expression suddenly turned dark.

"…And yet…I'm on my way…to do something awful, too…"

Anne whipped the horse again, and the wagon started rolling.

When she reached the center of the city, she called out to several children who were playing nearby and handed them some coins. She asked them to keep an eye on her wagon for a little while. The children happily accepted.

Anne alighted from her wagon and headed for the round plaza.

There, she found a disorderly collection of tents.

The tents were made of cloth varnished with animal tallow, and they had a distinctive greasiness to them. Underneath were rows of all sorts of wares, from foodstuffs to cloth to copper tools. It was a marketplace, bustling with shoppers.

A pungent sweet and sour smell tickled Anne's nose, drifting over from the tent where one could drink warm grape wine. From autumn through winter, it was a staple of the marketplace.

Anne passed through the crowded plaza, where people kept brushing shoulders, and emerged in an area with little pedestrian traffic.

This block was nearly deserted. There were plenty of shops set up but very few customers.

She looked at a nearby tent and saw several cages made of braided vines suspended from a horizontal bar.

Inside the cages were tiny fairies, each with only a single translucent wing on their back. Five or six of the cages hung in a row. The little fairies sitting inside regarded Anne with vacant eyes.

In an adjacent tent were three fairies covered in dense fur, about the size of puppies. They were bound together with chains linking their collars. Each had one wilted, transparent wing dangling from their back. The furry fairies bared their teeth and growled at Anne.

She was in the fairy marketplace.

Fairy hunters capture fairies in forests and fields and sell them to fairy dealers. The dealers pluck off one of each fairy's wings, and after determining a suitable price for each piece of merchandise, the captives are then put up for sale in the fairy markets.

For someone headed to the royal capital, going through Redington was out of the way. The reason Anne had stopped by despite the detour was because she knew the town had a reputable fairy market.

Anne approached one of the tents and addressed the fairy dealer.

"Excuse me, do you have any warrior fairies for sale?"

The dealer shook his head. "I haven't got any, no. Those things are dangerous."

"Well then, do you know of anyone in this market who does have warrior fairies?"

"Just one place. The old man in that tent by the wall has one, but I wouldn't recommend it, missy. It's defective."

"Is that so? Well, anyway, I'll go take a look. Thanks." Anne thanked the man and walked away.

Fairy dealers separate fairies into different categories for sale based on their abilities and appearances.

Most are sold for their labor as "worker fairies."

Fairies who are especially lovely or rare are sold as "pet fairies" to serve as living ornaments.

Fairies who are particularly violent are used as escorts and bodyguards, so they are sold as "warrior fairies."

Anne had come to the fairy market in order to purchase a warrior fairy.

After Redington, Anne was going to Lewiston to participate in the Royal Candy Fair.

The road that would take her from the western part of the kingdom, where Knoxberry and Redington were located, all the way to Lewiston was known as the Bloody Highway. It was a dangerous trail surrounded by wilderness, with no towns or villages along the way. Because the soil was poor, there were many bands of robbers driven by hunger, as well as countless wild beasts.

Even Emma had avoided the Bloody Highway on her travels.

There was another route, a safer road to Lewiston that one could follow by detouring to the south.

But that road wouldn't get Anne to her destination in time for that year's candy fair.

Anne wanted to make it there, no matter what it took. She knew her reasons were extremely sentimental, but if she didn't cling to them and continue toward her goal, her legs were liable to buckle beneath her.

I am definitely going to become a Silver Sugar Master this year. I've made up my mind.

She looked up with determination.

In order to go down the Bloody Highway, Anne would need a bodyguard.

Unfortunately, she had been unable to find anybody she could trust.

That left a warrior fairy as her only option. Fairies cannot disobey the master who holds their wing. As bodyguards, they are extremely reliable.

Anne's great wish was to become a Silver Sugar Master that year. In order to do so, she was prepared to bend her conviction not to enslave fairies.

When she got to the area the first dealer had pointed out, she stopped and looked around.

She wasn't sure which tent had the warrior fairy for sale.

The one to her left held palm-sized fairies in suspended cages. They were likely being sold as worker fairies.

The tent to her right had adorable fairies, about the size of a grain of wheat, inside glass bottles on a table. At that size, there was no way they could be workers, so they were probably pet fairies—sold to children to play with, like toys.

Then at the end of the row, directly in front of her, was a tent that had only one fairy for sale.

The tent had a sheet of leather spread out under it, and the fairy was sitting on top of the sheet with one knee bent. There were chains around his ankles, attached to an iron stake driven into the ground.

The fairy looked like a young man and appeared to be about two heads taller than Anne.

He had on black pants and boots and a loose cloak. The all-black outfit was probably something the fairy dealer had dressed him in to boost his selling price. With his outfit, this fairy stood out from the rest.

He had black eyes and black hair. There was an intense aura about him. His pale skin, which looked like it had never so much as seen sunlight, was characteristic of fairies.

Upon his back was one flexible, translucent wing. It gave the impression of a veil, spread out on the leather mat.

The fairy certainly looked beautiful. There was something undeniably noble about him.

Anne had no doubt that this was a pet fairy. He seemed like he would fetch a high price as an ornament for a rich noblewoman.

The fairy had his eyes cast downward under dark, sleek bangs. The languid afternoon sunlight danced across his eyelashes.

Just looking at him sent a shiver up Anne's spine.

The word beautiful *doesn't do him justice…*

Anne stared at the fairy, drawn in by those long eyelashes. Suddenly, he looked up.

Their eyes met, and the fairy stared directly at Anne.

He frowned for a moment, as if considering something. However, he seemed to quickly figure out whatever it was that had been perplexing him and mumbled, "I thought I knew you from somewhere. You look like a scarecrow."

He then abruptly averted his gaze from Anne, as if he had lost all interest.

"H…h-how rude… What a thing to say to a girl at the peak of her beauty!"

Anne clenched her fists in response to the fairy's words.

"Yours doesn't amount to much," the fairy said bluntly, still looking away.

"What was that—?!"

The person selling the rude fairy was an elderly fairy dealer. He sat smoking a pipe beside the tent.

When he saw Anne getting angry, the fairy dealer spoke up. He sounded exasperated. "Sorry about him, miss. This one's got a foul mouth. He says nasty things to anyone who walks by. Please don't pay him any mind."

"I do mind! This is probably none of my business, but you'll never sell a pet fairy with a sharp tongue like that! Maybe you should give up on selling him already and just let him go?!"

"He's no pet, miss. This here's a warrior fairy."

Anne's eyes went wide. It seemed this was the tent she had been told about, the one with the warrior fairy for sale.

But she couldn't believe it.

"A warrior fairy?! It can't be! The way he looks, it would be more appropriate to sell him as a pet. I've seen warrior fairies before. They were incredibly large and built like boulders."

"Well, he's a warrior, all right, and a fine specimen. Three fairy hunters died catching him."

Anne crossed her arms, openly suspicious. "The man over there said this fairy was defective. You say he's a warrior fairy, but maybe you're just making that up so you can off-load a foulmouthed pet fairy?"

"Reputation is a fairy dealer's most important asset. We don't lie."

Anne looked back at the fairy.

The fairy returned her gaze. He wore a faint smile, as if amused by something.

It was a bold expression to make. He certainly didn't look like an obedient fairy. He seemed the type to cause trouble, yet he didn't look strong enough to be useful as a warrior.

"I want to get a warrior fairy, but...you don't have any others besides him?" Anne asked.

The dealer shook his head. "Not many people deal in warrior fairies. You can only keep one at a time. He's the only one I have to sell. And I may as well tell you, I'm the sole dealer of warrior fairies in this market. But if you go to Ribonpool, sixty karons north of here, there's a merchant there who sells warrior fairies."

"If I detour all the way to Ribonpool, I won't make it in time for the Royal Candy Fair." Anne groaned, biting her thumbnail.

"Hey. Scarecrow," the fairy said abruptly.

Anne scowled at him.

"Scarecrow? I'm a maiden of fifteen, more vibrant than a flower! You can't possibly be talking about me?!"

"Is there anyone else here? Don't hesitate. Buy me."

Anne was stunned for a moment.

"...Buy you...? Was that...an order?"

Surprised, the fairy dealer put his hands on his belly and laughed.

"Incredible! That's the first time I've ever heard him tell someone to buy him. Did you fall in love with the young lady at first sight, boy? How 'bout this, miss? You've got no choice but to buy him now, right? I'll give you a great bargain, only one hundred cress. If he wasn't so crude, I would have sold him as a pet fairy. I bet someone would want him as one, even if I asked for three hundred cress."

"That's only if he didn't have a foul mouth, of course."

But the price the fairy dealer had suggested was certainly cheap. Warrior fairies and pet fairies are not very common, so they fetch high prices. One hundred cress is one piece of gold. Purchasing a warrior fairy for that price would be an incredible bargain.

"Listen, fairy. If you're bold enough to tell me to buy you, you must have confidence in your skills as a warrior, right?"

When Anne asked, a glint of light flashed across the fairy's eyes, and he looked up at her.

"What would you have me do?"

"Guard me. When I leave here, I'm headed for Lewiston, alone. I want you to protect me along the road."

The fairy smiled confidently. "Easy. And maybe while I'm at it, I could perform extra services. A kiss, perhaps?"

"Don't look so smug. I have no need of any such 'services.' And anyway, I would never give up my very first kiss so cheaply."

"So you're a child."

"Well, excuse me! For being a child!"

Anne certainly would have preferred a more serious, docile warrior fairy. But she didn't have time to make a detour to Ribonpool. Anne made up her mind.

There's no other choice!! He might be a little rude, but I can't afford to be picky.

She pulled out a little pouch from her dress pocket, opened it, and grabbed the single gold coin that was mixed in with all the copper.

"Mister, I'll buy this fairy."

"Heh-heh, you made up your mind, missy?" The dealer smiled, showing yellowed teeth.

Anne held out the gold coin, and the fairy dealer took and examined it. Then, he removed a small leather bag from around his neck.

"All right then, check the wing."

The fairy dealer opened the mouth of the little leather bag and pulled out something that looked like a transparent square of cloth, folded up to about the size of Anne's hand. He held the tip of it and gave it one good shake. When he did, the folded-up square gently unfurled.

A wing about as long as Anne was tall appeared before her eyes. It was so beautiful, she hesitated to touch it. As the light shifted, the transparent membrane shimmered a rainbow of colors. Despite having been folded like fine cloth, it retained no wrinkles or creases. Anne reached out to touch it gently and found it had a texture like silk. The softness made her shudder.

"This is his wing?"

"Sure is. Here, I'll prove it."

True to his word, the fairy dealer gripped the edge and the center of the wing and twisted it forcefully. The moment he did, the fairy under the tent groaned.

The warrior wrapped his arms around himself, and his whole body went stiff. He clenched his teeth.

"Stop!! I get it, that's enough!!"

At Anne's words, the dealer loosened his grip.

The fairy weakly put one hand on the ground. When he looked up, he glared hatefully at his captor.

The fairy dealer folded the wing back up, put it back into its bag, and handed it to Anne.

"Wear this around your neck, close to your body. And be careful. If this bag falls out of your hands, you don't know what the fairy might do. An acquaintance of mine accidentally let a warrior fairy in his employ steal their wing back and got himself killed. Warrior fairies are violent. That's why they're sold as such. If he gets his wing back, he's not going to just run away. There's a high chance he'll kill his master."

"But then what should I do when I'm sleeping? Won't he kill me in my sleep or something?"

"When you're turning in, make sure to hide the wing under your clothing and sleep holding it."

"And then I'll be all right?"

"Think about it. Imagine someone keeping a tight grip on your heart. If in the moment you killed them, that person squeezed and crushed your precious heart… Especially since fairy wings are so fragile, you see? They're scared and can't make any reckless moves. The idea of you hurting their wings terrifies fairies on an instinctual level. You saw the pain it caused this one just now, didn't you?"

Anne had indeed seen how he'd suffered, and she doubted that he'd be able to raise a hand against her.

However, Anne wasn't happy about the thought of controlling a fairy with fear and pain.

"Be careful, especially with this one. Up to now, every time I've tried to sell him, he's spat insults like you couldn't imagine out of that pretty mouth and angered the customer. I haven't been able to get rid of him. I don't know what kind of whim made him want you to buy him, but it's a miracle."

"Is he that much of a pain?!"

"You want to back out of the deal?"

Anne thought about it for a second, then shook her head.

"I don't have time to go to Ribonpool. I'll buy him."

"That's great. Handle the wing carefully. Whatever you do, don't let him get it back."

Anne nodded, and the fairy dealer unlocked the shackles on the fairy's ankles.

The fairy wore a faint, shrewd smile as he whispered to the dealer, "You just wait. Someday, I'll come back to kill you."

"That's fine. I look forward to the day."

Accepting the fairy's unsettling words of parting, the dealer finished removing his chains.

The fairy stood up. He was tall. His wing, reflecting the colors of a rainbow when it caught the sunlight, stretched down to the back of his knees.

"Now then, I bought you, so first of all, nice to meet you," Anne said.

The fairy smiled with his beautiful face. "You must be well-off if you're carrying gold around...scarecrow."

"Don't call me scarecrow! I'm Anne!"

The fairy dealer looked worried, watching their exchange.

"Miss, are you really gonna be able to handle him?"

"She can handle me. Right, scarecrow?" It was the fairy who answered.

When she saw him looking down on her mockingly, Anne shouted again, "My name is Anne! Anne Halford! Next time you call me scarecrow, you're gonna get it good!"

"...Looks like you'll be fine," the fairy dealer muttered.

Glaring at the fairy, Anne huffed through her nose as she replied, "Yes! I'll be fine! Don't you worry, old man. All right, you come with me."

"Say, what's your name?" Anne asked the fairy sitting next to her as she prodded the horse onward from atop her wagon.

Her bodyguard was leaning back against the wagon with his long legs drawn up and his arms folded across his chest, looking arrogant. Between Anne, who was busily handling the horse, and the fairy, the latter looked a hundred times more self-important.

The fairy glanced over at Anne as if she was a nuisance.

"What good will it do to tell you?"

"I mean, I don't know what to call you, do I?"

"You can call me Tom or Sam or whatever human-style name you like."

Normally, when a human acquires a fairy, the owner gives them a name. But Anne didn't want to do that. She thought being addressed by anything else must be humiliating.

"If it were me, I would want to be called by my real name. Don't you feel the same? I don't want to pick something random to call you. So tell me."

"I don't care what you call me. Don't ask such a silly thing. Give me whatever name you like. Call me anything."

The fairy looked away uncooperatively. Anne glanced over at his profile and said, "Fine, how about Crow?"

As one might expect, the fairy regarded Anne with an incredibly disagreeable expression.

"To get back at me for 'scarecrow'?"

"That's right. Crow."

The fairy frowned. After a moment of silence, he muttered, "Challe Fenn Challe."

"That's your name?"

The fairy nodded. Anne smiled.

"What a pretty name. It's much better than Crow. Challe Fenn Challe… Which part is your first name, and which part is your last name?"

"The whole thing is just…my name. Unlike with humans, there's no distinction between first and last names."

"Oh really? But Challe Fenn Challe is too long, so…I think I'll just call you Challe. Is that all right?"

"I told you to call me whatever you like. You are my master, aren't you?"

"Well…that's true."

Hearing that come out of the fairy's mouth again didn't make Anne feel good. She felt intensely guilty about purchasing and employing her own slave.

Anne steered her wagon away from the town of Redington. They were making progress toward the Bloody Highway.

The fields of wheat, with drooping heads ready for harvest, gradually gave way to sparse forest on either side of the road.

Sensing they were getting close to the Bloody Highway, Anne spoke up.

"Challe, I bought you so that I could have a bodyguard. But I'll make you a promise. If we make it down the Bloody Highway and arrive safely in Lewiston, I'll give you your wing back."

When he heard that, Challe looked at Anne suspiciously.

"Are you saying you'll release me?"

"Yes."

Challe looked stunned for a moment, but soon, he chuckled. "You're going to release a fairy you paid good money for? Is anyone really that naive?"

"It's rude to call me naive. I simply think that humans and fairies can be friends. I don't like the idea of putting a potential friend to work. I needed a reliable escort on very short notice, and having nowhere else to turn, I purchased you, Challe. But I don't want to use you if I don't have to. Of course, I don't want to sell you to another human, either. So I'm going to give your wing back. By making this promise, I hope to be able to treat you like any other friend accompanying me on a journey."

"Friend? We can't be friends."

Anne sighed at his cold response.

"You're probably right, but…it's just, that was something Mama and I believed. But ideals and dreams won't ever become reality if we don't act on them. So I'm doing just that, taking action."

"Your head really is as empty as a scarecrow's. I'll show you how foolish you're being once we get to Lewiston."

"I thought I told you not to call me a scarecrow?!"

Anne's hand flew through the air, but Challe easily dodged it. Anne bit her lower lip in frustration.

"If you think I'm so stupid, then why did you tell me to buy you? I wouldn't want to get ordered around by someone I thought was an idiot."

"All you humans are the same. It's easier on me to be under the control of a half-wit. And of all the humans I've had the misfortune of laying eyes on over the past few years, you seem by far the biggest fool."

"...Somehow...I feel really depressed after talking to you..."

Anne fully understood why Challe had remained unsold for so long.

She wasn't sure how she was going to endure being under his protection if he was going to verbally abuse her so badly.

The breeze fluttering the lace at her cuffs suddenly turned cold.

Anne recognized the rough, rocky road stretching out before them. It was the Bloody Highway. Her wagon rolled slowly onto it.

The tall, boxy wagon rocked back and forth as the wheels rolled over the stones.

The sky was a clear blue, but the air was cold. The Bloody Highway was surrounded by tall mountains, and the wind blowing down from them carried the chill of the heights with it.

As far as the eye could see, the land was a wilderness, rustling with dry, brown grass.

There were scattered stands of trees, but the soil was obviously barren.

There were no villages or towns along the Bloody Highway. The officials in charge of each province it passed through did maintain their respective sections, but that responsibility did not extend to controlling bandits or wild beasts along the path. There were only two actual requirements.

The first was to perform maintenance once per year to insure that plant life did not obstruct the road.

The second was to build a series of simple forts known as way stations, where travelers could make camp.

The Bloody Highway was dangerous, but those measures at least made it functional.

Anne possessed detailed maps of the whole kingdom. They were indispensable for travel, and Emma had always treated them with great care, adding new information as she went to make sure they were always up to date.

Anne could tell from the map of the western provinces that there was a way station nearby. The sun was setting, and she had to hurry to make it there. She somehow managed to arrive before sunset.

The way station was just a square courtyard surrounded by tall stone walls in the middle of a copse of trees. There was no roof. The gate housed an iron door that could be raised and lowered using chains. The overgrown grassy area inside was spacious, with enough room to fit five horse-drawn wagons at night.

In short, travelers could take refuge behind the walls, hiding themselves from bandits and beasts.

Anne parked her wagon in the way station and pulled the iron door closed behind her.

She was understandably exhausted from being jolted around on a wagon for the first time in six months, and she decided to go to bed early.

Anne pulled out two of the leather mats and blankets that she kept stuffed under the seat of the wagon. One set was for her, and she spread that one out beside the wagon. She handed the other set to Challe.

"You can choose where you want to sleep. Lay that out for bedding. And here's dinner. Sorry it's not much, but we can't afford luxury while we're traveling."

Next, Anne handed Challe a wooden cup full of grape wine and a single apple.

Dinner was frugal, in consideration of future travel.

Anne wrapped herself up in her blanket and bit into her apple, which she finished in seconds. Flinging the core as far as she could, she downed her wine in one gulp. As the bitter liquid hit her stomach, it immediately transformed into warmth. She felt her ears growing hot as she curled up on her leather mat.

Challe spread his mat out a short distance from Anne and sat down, placing the blanket over his lap. He held his cup of wine in his hand and looked up at the moon.

It was a full moon that night. The silver glow illuminated Challe's face.

Bathed in moonlight, the fairy's beauty was enhanced all the more. He had the luster of a precious gem wet with dew.

The translucent wing on his back glimmered with a peaceful, pale-green color.

Unlike the one that had been torn off, the wing on Challe's back seemed to subtly change color and sheen based on his mood.

I wonder if they're cold? Or are they warm?

Anne felt an overwhelming desire to touch it.

"Fairies' wings are so beautiful. Could I touch yours?"

Anne reached out her hand as she asked. When she did, a shudder ran through Challe's wing, which made a faint sound as it shook. Then it flapped, beating the grass two or three times.

Anne retracted her hand in surprise and saw Challe's sharp eyes looking her way.

"Don't touch! You may hold the other, but this one's mine."

Challe's cold rage reminded Anne that she held his other wing hostage and that, to fairies, their wings were as precious as life itself.

"I'm sorry. I… That was thoughtless of me."

Anne apologized meekly and gripped the strings of the leather bag dangling on her chest.

Fairies' wings are the source of their life force. They are what hearts are to humans. Anne had another person's heart in her hands, and she was threatening to crush it if he didn't follow her orders.

That was what Anne was doing. From a fairy's perspective, her actions must have seemed entirely monstrous.

Anne sighed softly.

I shouldn't do things like that.

She wondered if she could get Challe to listen to her requests without resorting to such behavior.

Maybe if I could befriend him? If I did that, there would be no need to order him around.

She wondered if there was any way to get him to cooperate with her requests of his own volition.

"Hey, Challe? I've got a proposal," Anne said, sitting up a bit. "I mentioned it this afternoon, but couldn't we try to be friends?"

"Are you stupid?"

Challe answered dismissively and turned away.

Anne dejectedly covered her head with her blanket.

I guess it's impossible right away. But I have a feeling that if I treat him well and with sincerity, he'll understand in time. Anyway, I wonder what he was thinking about when he was looking up at the moon? His eyes looked so bright…

Anne's eyelids grew heavy, and she drifted off to sleep.

In the pleasant darkness, Anne had a dream.

In it, she was camping out under the stars as usual.

Anne was wrapped up in her blanket, and Emma was going in and out of the wagon, working busily.

Anne breathed a sigh of relief when she saw her mother there before her eyes. With that relief came a single line of hot tears streaming down her cheek.

"My, my, what's wrong, Anne? Are you in pain?"

"No, I had a terrible dream. An awful nightmare that you died, Mama."

"You silly thing. If you had such a scary dream, you must not be feeling very well. Let me check your temperature."

Emma's cold fingers gently probed Anne's forehead. Her mother's fingers had always been slender and cool. It was because she chilled them in water when working with silver sugar, which melted quickly.

Those fingers seemed unbearably lovely and ephemeral. Without thinking, Anne grasped them tightly.

"Mama, please. Don't go!"

Anne woke with a start, roused by her own shouting.

She realized she had been dreaming. But the fingers Anne had grasped were real. She saw Challe's face, which was so close that she could feel his breath. His black hair was nearly brushing her cheek.

"Wh-what?!"

She pushed his hand away and sprang up.

Don't tell me this is more of that smug extra "service" of his?!

Challe smirked and got up. His smile was cold.

Anne realized that this was unlikely to be the service Challe had suggested.

What on earth was he…? Just now, he was going for my neck…

"Were you…?"

At that moment, Anne noticed that the leather strap hanging around her neck was sticking out of her collar—the strap of the bag containing Challe's wing.

"Challe. Don't tell me…you were trying to steal your wing back?"

"I almost had it, too," he said, without a hint of shame.

"So you were trying to steal it? How mean…"

"How so?"

"I told you, didn't I? I want to be your friend, Challe. And yet…"

Anne honestly wanted to befriend Challe. She felt he had betrayed her in spite of that, which made her sad.

Challe looked at Anne moping and chuckled. "You want to be my friend? The kind of friend who holds my life in her hands?"

His words startled her.

"You purchased me. You're putting me to work. We can never be friends."

If Anne was really going to put her ideals into practice, she would have to return the wing, ask for Challe's companionship, and then seek his cooperation. That was what she would have to do.

But she was frankly afraid to return his wing. So Anne held his life in her hands while claiming she wanted to be friends. Even she had to admit it was selfish. Given that was the nature of their relationship, they could never be friends.

As long as Anne held Challe's wing, she was his master.

Challe had just been trying to reclaim his wing from his captor. It was only natural for a fairy like him.

Anne was wrong to feel betrayed.

As Challe's master, Anne had simply been childish and careless enough to give him the opportunity.

"…I am a fool, aren't I?"

Anne sighed softly. She had only imagined that she wanted to be friends to make herself feel more comfortable. She realized how insensitive and stupid she had been.

"I have to go to Lewiston. It's too dangerous a gamble to give you your wing back and then ask you to protect me until we get there. That's why

I was determined to hire you, but in a way, I was naive. Telling you I wanted to become friends...was a dumb thing to say."

Anne closed her eyes and took a deep breath. She then reopened them.

"If I can get you to cooperate with me so I can make it safely to Lewiston, then I'll return your wing. You can't trust that I'll keep my promise, so you tried to steal it back, right? Or was it because you can't stand being controlled by a human, even for a short while? Either way is fine, but I'm not going to be so careless going forward, so forget about it."

Anne looked up at the fairy, who wore a blank expression. He didn't respond.

"While I'm at it, let me add that I'm still going to keep my promise. Once we get to Lewiston, I'll return your wing. After that, I'll ask you to be my friend for real. Until then, I am your master."

Challe snorted and turned his back. The wing on his back reflecting the moonlight was pitifully lonesome.

He looked up at the evening sky and mused, "What a beautiful moon."

I failed.

Challe Fenn Challe was looking up at the moon, but he could feel Anne's presence as she lay behind him. He could tell how tense she was. In that state, even if she fell asleep again, she was liable to wake just feeling him approach. It would be impossible to attempt to steal his wing again that night.

However, he was not impatient.

Challe had fallen into the hands of a fairy hunter and been sold from human to human.

He always spent his time fantasizing about killing his master and fleeing. He thought of nothing else.

But it wasn't that easy. The humans he had known were cruel and wary.

When he was put up for sale in the fairy market in Redington, he decided to get himself purchased by the most idiotic human possible. He figured that if he was bought by some blockhead, he could kill them or maybe take his wing back without them noticing, then make his escape.

Except all the customers interested in warrior fairies seemed shrewd and ruthless. So every time the fairy dealer tried to bargain with a customer, Challe hurled the nastiest abuse and angered every one of them.

He had been sitting under the stall, wondering what kind of customer would show up that day, hoping they were moronic, when suddenly, he caught a whiff of a sweet scent. It reminded him of the aroma of silver sugar.

When he looked up, there was a skinny girl with hair the color of barley staring down at him.

The girl had said she wanted to buy a warrior fairy. It was a golden opportunity.

The moment Anne decided to purchase him, Challe had smiled to himself.

A childish little girl who talked nonsense about treating fairies like friends and becoming pals and so on. He wouldn't even have to soil his blade with her blood. He'd imagined that he could simply steal his wing.

Yet Anne had proven herself more perceptive than he'd thought.

When he failed to steal his wing back, Challe had resigned himself to some sort of punishment, some torture inflicted on his captive wing.

But Anne hadn't punished him. Far from it, she'd repeated her promise that she would return his wing once they reached Lewiston, insisting she would become his friend after she did.

It was strange. He didn't know what she was thinking. But—

No matter what it is, she's an idiot.

With such a naive young girl, Challe was sure to have plenty of opportunities. He was in no hurry.

For nearly seventy years, he had been under the continuous control of humans. He didn't care whether his freedom was one day away or three.

Suddenly, he smelled that sweet scent again. He glanced behind him. Sure enough, the aroma was coming from Anne's hair and fingertips. The smell of silver sugar stirred his memories and awakened his senses.

Challe unconsciously put his fingers to his mouth. He imagined a sweet sensation that he had known in the distant past. The pleasure of having his wings gently stroked. Gentle hands. His body recalling the feeling, he let out an involuntary sigh.

Liz…

Behind him, Anne turned over in her sleep. Startled by her movement, Challe pulled his fingers away from his lips.

He glanced over his shoulder at Anne. Her eyes were closed.

"Mama, please. Don't go!"

Anne had shouted those words earlier before waking. Challe suddenly felt suspicious about that.

Who is making a child like this travel alone? What is that mother of hers doing?

The hand that had gripped Challe's fingers felt very fragile.

For some reason, the feeling of her touch stuck in his mind.

Chapter 2

REUNION ON THE BLOODY HIGHWAY

There are no villages or towns along the Bloody Highway, which spans about twelve hundred karons.

Anne wondered whether she would be able to traverse it safely.

She glanced at Challe, who sat next to her on the wagon.

He had a beautiful face. She had never seen such an elegant warrior fairy before, and that worried her.

She wondered if Challe would actually be useful as a warrior.

Now that I've purchased him, all I can do is trust him, but…

The Royal Candy Fair was only half a month away. It would take them nine days to cross the Bloody Highway.

Once they arrived in Lewiston, Anne would have five days to prepare before the candy fair commence. It was going to be close.

They had set off at dawn but had just barely started down the highway. They still had a long way to go, and their time was limited.

Anne wanted to get as much distance behind them as possible during the day, when it was still relatively safe.

From time to time, she identified black shapes that looked like packs of wolves up on distant crags, but they showed no signs of coming down from the mountains.

The pair made fine progress down the road until early afternoon.

It was a few hours until sunset.

Anne expected them to reach the next way station, where she had decided to spend the second night, with time to spare.

When they got there, they would be two hundred karons from the start of the highway, one-sixth of the way through their journey.

As the wagon cruised on through the quiet, monotonous scenery, the sound of horses whinnying suddenly filled Anne's ears. At the same time, the high-pitched clang of steel striking steel pierced the air.

Startled, Anne yanked on the reins. As the wagon slowed to a stop, she looked toward the source of the commotion.

Just ahead on the road, there was a big cloud of dust.

In the center of it was a brand-new boxy wagon. Its back was to Anne, so she couldn't spot the driver. She could, however, just make out a hand wielding a sword on the other side of it.

Surrounding the carriage were ten men on horses, riding round and round in circles, whooping and hollering loudly. They were all dressed differently, but each had a bit of cloth tied around their head, concealing their identity. They were bandits targeting travelers.

"Oh no!"

The blood drained from Anne's face. She knew that if she encountered bandits, just escaping would be considered a victory. She shouldn't even try to help whoever was already under attack. She could see the outcome with her own eyes.

All travelers understood that rule and did not resent one another for following it.

In this situation, the most sensible thing for her to do would be to take refuge in a way station. But the way station where they'd spent the previous night was far behind them.

Anne looked on either side of the road for a place to hide, but the surrounding area was filled with only empty fields of long grasses. There were no tall trees nearby and nowhere to hide a whole wagon.

As she was looking around, two of the riders in the ring of bandits stopped circling.

They seemed to have noticed Anne's wagon and turned their horses' heads toward her.

"Oh no, they're coming this way!!"

Anne shrieked and grabbed at Challe's sleeve. She then finally remembered something.

"H-hey, you!! Listen, Challe! You are a warrior fairy, right? Drive those bandits away!"

Challe looked at Anne wearily. "What a pain…"

"We're in danger! Please!!"

As she pleaded with him, Challe grabbed Anne's wrist and pulled her hand off his sleeve. Instead, he snatched her arm and jerked her toward him.

"Challe?! Wh-what?"

Challe brought his face close to hers and coaxed, "Don't ask me to do it. You're supposed to command me, right?"

Despite the situation, Anne's gaze was drawn to the long lashes framing Challe's eyes as he peered into hers. His voice was oddly sensual.

"Uh, too close! Hey, you're too close, Challe!! Back up! Just go fight!"

Blood rushed to Anne's face. It was no time to be blushing, but she couldn't hide her agitation.

"Your face is red."

"J-j-j-just go, please!"

"How amusing." Challe chuckled condescendingly. Without a doubt, he was toying with her.

"Challe! Go now, please!"

"I told you, you've got to order me."

"Order you?! Look, they're coming!"

"*Go now, or I'll tear your wing.* If you command me like that, I'll go at once."

"What are you talking about?! It doesn't matter—just go!"

Anne was frightened, and she wasn't used to commanding fairies. She totally forgot that she was in possession of Challe's wing, his very life.

"Command me."

Anne squeezed her eyes shut so she couldn't see Challe's beautiful face. And then—— "I said go! If you don't go, I'll hit you!!"

She issued the most violent order she could muster.

When he heard it, Challe shrugged.

"Well…all right, then. Here I go. As you command, mistress scarecrow."

Challe let go of Anne's arm and jumped down lightly from the wagon.

He walked slowly toward the approaching horsemen.

He casually stretched the palm of his right hand out in front of his chest and narrowed his eyes, almost like he was smiling. The single wing on his back shuddered slightly. The wilted wing unfurled slowly. One section of it caught the sunlight and shone an assortment of colors.

From all around Challe, sparkling beads of light started streaming toward his open palm.

Before Anne's eyes, the beads of light condensed, forming a long, thin shape that turned into a sword that radiated a silvery gleam.

A sword...?! He can do that?! Then Challe really is—

Challe gripped the newly formed blade. He held it down at his side.

—a warrior fairy!

Suddenly, Challe broke into a run.

He was quieter than the wind, not making a single sound as he raced with his body low to the ground.

In the blink of an eye, he was within reach of the approaching horses and swung his sword at their legs.

In a single stroke, he simultaneously lopped off both of the horses' front legs. When their mounts suddenly collapsed, the two bandits were thrown violently to the ground.

Without even watching his first two targets fall, Challe dashed over to the rest of the riders.

The other bandits noticed Challe, but no sooner had they turned to look in his direction than the swordsman lopped off their horses' legs, too, one after another. Five more horses fell to the ground.

There were three bandits left on horseback. They shouted angrily and slashed at Challe.

One of them swung a sword down at him, and Challe lopped off his assailant's whole arm.

Their leader blanched. "Retreat!! Retreat!!" he shouted, turning his horse back toward the foothills.

The bandits who had been thrown to the ground stumbled after him. Even the man who'd lost his arm spurred his horse with a desperate expression on his face, groaning as he retreated.

The cloud of dust quickly blew away, revealing the seven writhing horses with their legs severed, as well as the three corpses of bandits who'd died on impact when their mounts went down. The air was deadly silent.

Challe nimbly twirled his sword, shaking off the blood. Then, he deliberately thrust his blade into each of the struggling horses' necks, ending their lives one after another.

Anne's fingers felt cold and were trembling slightly.

She averted her eyes, trying not to look at the horses that Challe had put out of their misery. Given the severity of their injuries, there was no way to save them. It was much more compassionate to kill them than allow them to suffer needlessly.

Even though she understood that, Anne still couldn't bring herself to look at them directly.

Indeed, Anne had been the one who'd insisted Challe help the people in the other wagon.

But she had never expected her command would result in the deaths of seven horses and three humans, all in the blink of an eye. A single word from her, and three men were dead, bandits though they were.

Anne was filled with surprise and fear at the thought that her orders could bring about such results.

So this is a warrior fairy...

While she was momentarily frozen in place, the driver of the boxy wagon ahead of her got down from his seat.

Anne recognized the other driver, making her doubt her own eyes.

"It can't be... Jonas?!"

Jonas stood in a daze as he watched Challe put the horses down, and at the sound of Anne's voice, he looked up.

"......Huh? ......Anne?"

Once he'd finished killing all the horses, Challe held his sword by his side. Just like when he'd formed the blade, it gradually turned into beads of light and dispersed.

Anne quickly drove her wagon forward, steering around the bodies of the horses and bandits who'd been mercilessly slaughtered. She tried to look at them as little as possible.

When her wagon was in line with Jonas's, she pulled to a stop.

Anne hopped out of the driver's seat and rushed to Jonas.

"What are you doing here, Jonas?!"

"Anne! Is he your warrior fairy?! Then that means you're the one who saved me?! Ah! This must be fate! Anyway, I'm glad I found you! You set out half a day before me, so I thought you'd be much farther along."

Jonas seemed excited, and he grasped both of Anne's hands tightly in his.

"I stopped by Redington, so… Wait, that doesn't matter. Why are you in a place like this, Jonas?"

"I followed you. It's dangerous to let you travel alone, so I persuaded my parents, readied a carriage, and followed you. I'm going with you."

"Why?!"

"Why…? I only need one reason. You must know how I feel about you."

Anne was stunned by his words.

"Huh?"

"I love you, Anne. I want to go with you."

"Um…Jonas… I'm very happy to hear that, but…"

Anne gently pulled her hands from his grip and moved away.

"But, Jonas, I think you're badly mistaken when it comes to your feelings for me. Surely, you can't have fallen for me. There's just no way. I think you're confusing the pity you feel toward me with love."

Anne's appearance was quite plain, and she didn't go out of her way to be charming.

She had never thought of herself as appealing.

In fact, although Jonas and Anne had spent half a year in close quarters, their relationship was still more distant than even a simple friendship.

Yet Jonas had proposed to marry her, despite the distance between them.

Anne could think of no reason why he would do that, except out of pity for a girl who had just lost her mother.

She was sure Jonas must have felt sorry for her and confused that feeling for love, mistakenly concluding that he was head over heels for her.

"It's not pity. I love you, Anne. Say, you're taking part in the Royal Candy Fair in Lewiston, right? You told me you were. In that case, I'm going, too. I'll protect and support you so you can become a Silver Sugar Master."

"Wait. You were attacked by bandits just a moment ago; you can't possibly protect me, can you?! Besides, aren't you heir to your family's candy store? And isn't there a possibility of you becoming the maestro of the Radcliffe Workshop?! I can't let someone important like you accompany me on such a dangerous journey. What if you get hurt? I'd never be able to face the Anders family, and after they took care of me, too."

"The bandits were, well… I let my guard down a little. I'm a man; I'll be fine."

"What are you basing that on?!"

"It's fine. I'll be fine. I have a sword, too."

"Hey, are you listening to me?"

"Besides, Mother and Father agreed I should accompany you to Lewiston."

"The Anders agreed to that? I doubt it. Anyway, go home."

"I can't turn back now. The danger is the same, whether I turn around or continue."

In his ardor, Jonas sounded frantic, like someone delirious with fever.

Anne was certain he had completely misinterpreted his feelings.

She knew her conscience would never rest easy if she ended up leading poor, lovestruck Jonas to his death.

"No way. You have to go back."

"Anne, don't be so cold. Come on."

Jonas smiled and gripped Anne's hand again.

It startled her, and though she tried to pull away, he kept a firm grip on her.

"I came for you. Do you hate me? Are you not happy?"

Anne was flummoxed by his gaze. All the girls back in the village were crazy about his kind, smiling face.

"I don't hate you. But—but listen. How do I put this? That's not the issue…"

Challe didn't seem inclined to interrupt Anne and Jonas's exchange. He had been leaning against the back of the wagon the whole time, looking up at the sky. However, he suddenly scowled and stood up straight.

"Scarecrow. Let's get moving quickly. The wolves will be here once they catch the scent of blood. Look up."

Anne and Jonas looked up at the sky. The silhouettes of three black birds circled overhead.

"Crows. The cleaners of the wastelands. Once they appear, the wolves aren't far behind."

Anne nodded quickly. Jonas's grip slackened, and she pulled her own hand back from his.

"Got it. We'll depart immediately. Jonas, please turn back from here."

"No. I'm going."

"Listen, Jonas. If you die, your parents will be very sad, and the village girls will cry buckets. If you're not around, who will inherit your shop? There are a lot of things in this world that matter to you, aren't there? You have to protect that," Anne said kindly.

Jonas stared directly back at her. "I'm going, even if you tell me not to. My parents have nothing to do with this. The shop, too—it's irrelevant to me right now. The only thing that's important to me at the moment are my feelings for you."

Jonas had a warm home to go back to. He had two parents and even a shop to inherit. He carried a lot of important expectations on his shoulders. He wasn't an orphan like Anne, without a single soul to cry over him if he died. There was no need for him to face the same dangers.

Despite all that, he didn't seem to understand the value of everything he had.

Anne was at a complete loss in the face of Jonas's obstinacy.

"At any rate, you're not someone who ought to be taking such risks."

Anne turned her back on him and quickly climbed up into the driver's seat of her wagon.

Challe was already sitting there. He looked sidelong at Anne's worried expression as she spurred the horse on.

Challe smirked.

"So you've got boys chasing after you? Not bad for a little girl."

"I am not a little girl! I am fifteen. An adult! And besides, it's not like that with Jonas. He just feels sorry for me, that's all. I can't believe he's going to put himself in danger for that."

As she spoke, Anne's attention was drawn to what was happening behind her.

Jonas boarded his own wagon and set off slowly, following Anne and Challe. It didn't seem like he planned to return home.

After all, now that he was on the highway, it was as Jonas had said: He would face the same danger whether he turned back or continued.

"What am I gonna do…?" Anne grumbled. She then mumbled a few words to Challe. "That wagon behind us… Would you please go help him out if anything happens?"

Anne did not hate Jonas. On the contrary, she liked his kind smile and amiable manner. Plus, she thought he must be a good person if he had so much sympathy for someone that he confused it for love.

She couldn't just abandon him.

"If you want to make me do something, you'll have to give me an order. After all, you've got my wing."

"You were trying to get me to order you around earlier, too. Why are you so persistent about that?"

"I don't intend to do a single thing unless I've been ordered to."

In short, Challe was saying he wouldn't lift a finger unless Anne threatened to take his life if he failed to follow her orders. Put it another way, he would only obey her if she resorted to threats.

He was resolved to not follow any trivial commands, such as *Look after the horse for a minute* or *Grab that blanket.*

Anne didn't like the idea of having to threaten to kill him just to get him to hand her a blanket.

She sighed at the fact that he was so hard to handle.

"Last night, I resolved to put you to use, Challe. But when it comes down to it, I don't want to order you around in such a nasty way. So I'm going to ask. For the time being, I'm going to keep asking you instead. But if you tell me no, my requests will turn into orders. If it's what you'd like, I'll order you to do my bidding unless you want your wing to be torn to bits. I'm prepared to do that. But I'm going to ask nicely first."

Challe listened to Anne's words, staring at her unblinkingly.

"You really are a strange scarecrow."

"Challe, you choose the worst moments to call me a scarecrow, you know? …Well, whatever, it's fine… I can be a scarecrow."

Anne wondered what she ought to do if anything should happen to Jonas. Just thinking about that seemed like it would give her a headache, though, and she lacked the energy to come up with a reply to Challe's scarecrow remark.

Anne stopped her wagon. When she did, Jonas pulled to a stop alongside her as well.

The two of them were looking up at the way station where Anne had decided to spend the second night of her journey.

"So this is a way station, huh? I've never actually stayed in one before tonight."

"It's your first time? Then what did you do last night?"

"Actually, I had guards accompanying me up until this afternoon. There were some men working rough jobs on the outskirts of Knoxberry Village, and I asked them to escort me. So last night, I parked the carriage on the side of the road and slept in the cargo hold. The guards protected me all night, but..."

"But?"

"Apparently, they realized I had money hidden somewhere in the carriage. Just before noon today, they turned their swords on me, stole the money, and ran off."

Jonas was fairly nonchalant as he related this. He was either braver than he looked or really laid-back.

Anne's shoulders slumped.

"That is unfortunate, but...aren't you going too easy on the guards?"

"Well, probably, yeah. But as long as things work out in the end, everything's fine. They spared my life, after all. And because of that, I was able to run into you!"

Jonas didn't seem to have the slightest idea about the dangers of traveling.

Anne knew she would be in trouble if she didn't instill some sense in him, especially if he was planning to tag along with her.

"Jonas. After we stay here tonight, you have to turn back tomorrow, okay?"

"I'm just going where I want to go! I'm not necessarily following you."

"Now see here. Jonas—"

"Come on, let's go."

Jonas winked and spurred his horse on. Anne put her hand on her forehead.

"Aah…my head hurts…"

Anne and Jonas drove their wagons into the way station and shut the iron door behind them.

Once they were inside, Jonas discretely pulled his wagon over alongside the wall. Then, he immediately went inside the boxy cargo hold. It looked like he planned to sleep there. The fact that he didn't park close to Anne's wagon seemed like his way of asserting his independence.

Anne made a fire beside her wagon. She then poured water into a pot and added dried meat and scraps of vegetables to make a simple soup. When it was done, she glanced over at Jonas's wagon.

Because it was autumn, the temperature did drop at night. She felt awkward about being the only one with something hot to eat.

Anne put some soup in a wooden bowl and walked over to the back of Jonas's wagon.

She knocked gently on the doors.

"Jonas? It's me, open up."

She heard some kind of rustling from inside, and before long, one of the doors opened.

"Do you need something?"

The one who'd opened it was a female fairy about the size of Anne's palm. Her single wing fluttered strenuously as she clung to the door handle.

This was Cathy, a worker fairy employed by the Anders family. She had flaming-red hair. She lifted her primly raised nose even higher into the air and glared at Anne with her big, upturned eyes.

"Cathy?! You came with Jonas?"

"I have always been Master Jonas's personal fairy servant. Of course I came."

"Is that so? Then where is Jonas?"

"The master is resting."

"Well then, I'll hand this over to you. Can you tell him to eat the soup when he wakes up?"

Cathy looked at Anne's extended arm and smirked.

"Such crude fare. I doubt Master Jonas will eat it."

Cathy was the very image of a servant working for a high-ranking master, the kind who wore the mantle of her master's authority and misused it to look down on others. Anne frowned.

"That may be true at home, but we should be grateful for even simple food when we're on the road."

Cathy made a disgusted face, but she descended lightly to the floor and held out both hands.

Fairies who have had one wing removed cannot truly fly. It is impossible for them to hover in midair. Consequently, Cathy had no option but to drop to the floor to take the bowl.

Anne leaned over and passed it to her.

To Cathy, the soup bowl was as big as a washbasin. Her face twisted into a grimace as she grabbed hold of it.

"It stinks like animal grease. Even a fairy like me wouldn't touch it!"

"Ohhh, sooo sorry! Guess I shouldn't have bothered!"

Fuming, Anne walked back to the fireside and violently stirred the contents of the pot.

Challe was sitting there, idly staring into the flames.

Anne picked up another bowl and poured some soup for Challe. She then wordlessly held the bowl out to him.

Challe stared unblinkingly at the soup before him before regarding Anne curiously.

"What am I supposed to do with this...?"

Anne glared back at him furiously.

"Do you think I'm handing you this because I want you to spoon-feed it to me?! It's your portion, Challe—obviously! Am I so wrong for giving you some?! Or does this greasy pauper's soup also offend your palate?!"

Challe looked surprised by Anne's flare-up.

"What's wrong with you all of a sudden? It's like your head is on fire or something."

"And I guess it'll burn well, since I've got the head of scarecrow!"

Challe couldn't suppress his laughter. Then, with a mellow expression, he stretched out his hand for the bowl being offered to him.

"Looks like someone's quite fired up."

"I'm angry. A fairy just told me that humble soup like this isn't good enough for the precious heir to a candy shop. Do you hate a meager meal like this, too?!"

"I wasn't rejecting your soup. I was just…surprised."

Challe accepted the bowl and held it in both hands.

"Surprised? By what? I guess because it looked disgusting or something…?"

"I was surprised that you offered soup to me before serving yourself."

"Why? It's only proper for the person serving the meal to feed everyone before serving herself, right? It's a matter of good manners. Here's your spoon."

Anne was about to hand Challe a utensil for his soup, but she noticed the portion had already decreased by half.

"Challe, you haven't taken a bite yet, have you? Is there a hole in your bowl, maybe?"

"I ate it."

"You ate it?! How?!"

"Fairies don't eat with our mouths. We hold food in our hands or just touch it, then we absorb it."

As Anne stared at the bowl in Challe's hands, the liquid surface of the soup gradually lowered, undulating slightly. It looked like it was rapidly evaporating.

"Can you…taste it?" Anne asked reflexively as she stared at the disappearing broth.

"No. Even if I eat something, I can't taste it."

"So fairies can't taste anything at all?! That means that no matter what you eat, you have no way of enjoying it?"

"There is one thing we can taste. Just one."

"What?"

"Silver sugar… It's sweet."

Challe cast his eyes downward, as if lost in a memory. His expression looked terribly lonely. Anne thought that whatever he was remembering must have been painful.

She wondered what sort of life this sarcastic fairy had led before he was enslaved and put up for sale at the market.

Her heart hurt to imagine it.

Born in nature to live a carefree life, only to be flushed out, hunted down, and then sold. How would that feel? Anne imagined that if such a thing had happened to her, the anger and resentment would have hardened her heart.

"Do you like silver sugar or hate it?"

"I don't hate it."

"Then I'll make some candy for you! I am a budding candy crafter, you know!"

"You are?"

Challe gave Anne a doubtful sidelong glance. She puffed out her chest a little.

"You don't know the half of it! My mother was a Silver Sugar Master. As her daughter, I've been making things out of silver sugar since I was a toddler. I'm quite skilled, if I do say so myself. I think I'll make a candy in the shape of a moonflower. That would suit you."

Anne figured it probably wasn't any fun eating food you couldn't taste. The thought filled her with a desire to make something for him.

If Challe's heart had grown cold, the gentle sweetness of sugar candy might soften it just a little.

A look of confusion passed over Challe's face. She found his vexed expression somewhat endearing.

Anne stood up with a smile and walked around to the rear of her own wagon. The moment she placed her hands on the two doors there—

Bang! She heard the sound of something ricocheting around inside the carriage, and the whole vehicle shook violently.

Anne jumped away at once and shrieked, "Challe!"

She leaped back to Challe's side, grabbing at his sleeve.

"S-something is inside the carriage! Go look. Take a look, please!"

Challe glanced over at Anne.

"Is that an order?"

"O-order?"

"Will you tear up my wing if I don't?"

"I wasn't planning to, but—"

"Do it yourself, then."

"Aaah, you're the worst!!"

Anne hated the vulgarity of threatening to tear Challe's wing. It made it difficult for her to order him around.

Challe saw right through Anne and insisted that she command him. That much was clear from the contemptuous look on his face. He planned to resist until the very end.

Anne felt like a fool for pitying him even for a second.

She had lost her cool, and her anger made her feel less afraid.

"Fine! I'll check it out!"

Anne had spent fifteen years traveling the kingdom with nobody but her mother, and she was sure she had more courage than the average fifteen-year-old girl.

She picked up a piece of unused firewood and approached the doors to the cargo hold.

Wielding the stick in one hand, she slowly opened one door.

Inside the wagon, it was quiet.

The interior of the boxy wagon was tall enough for a person to stand and walk around. High windows near the ceiling on each side let in bright moonlight, faintly illuminating the hold.

Set against one the walls was a workbench. Atop it was a stone slab used for kneading sugar candy, a wooden spatula, and a scale, and lined up in an orderly row were vials of coloring powder extracted from various plants.

On the opposite side, five casks stood against the wall.

The interior of the carriage looked the same as always.

"There's…nothing here?"

Anne timidly stuck her head inside and looked around. The moment she did—

"Hey, you!!"

With a high-pitched yell, a small silhouette leaped out at her from underneath the workbench.

"Kyaaaaaaaaaaaah!!"

Anne screamed and swung the stick as hard as she could.

She landed a direct hit on the thing speeding toward her.

The force of the strike sent it flying right out the doors of the wagon, where it crashed into the back of Challe's head as he sat by the fire.

Challe turned to face his attacker with a scowl. He picked up the little figure that had plopped to the ground behind him after the impact.

Gripping the projectile tightly, he shouted angrily at Anne, "You hit me! What is this?!"

Anne was just as confused and shouted right back, "I don't know!! It was inside the carriage!"

"It's…?"

Challe turned his attention to the thing he was holding. Then he frowned.

"Let go of me, you big jerk!! Who do you take me for?!" the little silhouette protested in a high-pitched voice.

The figure kicking and struggling against Challe's grip on the scruff of his neck was a sweet-looking young male fairy with silver hair. He had only one wing on his back. Strangely, he had the other wing wrapped around his neck like a scarf.

"Let me go!"

"Shut up."

Challe released him, and the small fairy crashed to the ground with a shout.

"Tch. Reckless jerk. I'm delicate; you ought to treat me more gently."

Rubbing his backside, the little fairy stood up.

Anne approached him cautiously and knelt, peering down at the newcomer.

The fairy looked up at Anne with big, round blue eyes.

"So you were the one making a fuss in the carriage?"

"I wasn't making a fuss. I dozed off and had a bad dream. I'm very sensitive, so it sent me flying. I flew too high and bumped into the ceiling, that's all."

"Uh-huh…you really flew up hard… At any rate, who are you? When did you get into my wagon and why?"

"I am Mithril Lid Pod, and I came to return a favor."

"Return a favor?"

"From yesterday. You saved me. So I've come to repay my debt."

When he said that, Anne finally recognized him.

"Oh! It's you! The one the fairy hunter in Redington was picking on?"

During their first encounter, he had been covered in mud, so she hadn't seen much of his face. Thinking back carefully, though, she did recognize his shrill voice.

She had no doubt that the wing around the fairy's neck was the same one she had retrieved from the fairy hunter.

"That's right. I spotted your carriage in Redington and snuck onboard so I could pay you back for everything. I thought I could do it right away, but, well…that big moron in Redington worked me hard and wore me out. I fell asleep by mistake. I've been sleeping until just now. But thanks to that, I've got plenty of energy! I'm going to pay you back in full, starting immediately!"

"But back then, didn't you tell me you weren't going to say thanks to a human?"

"Sure did! But it's a fact that you saved me. I'm not a heartless creature like you humans, so I'm going to repay you, even if I don't want to. Let me just say this: I'll repay the favor, but I'll never say thanks as long as I live! Got it?"

The fairy thrust his little pointer finger sternly at Anne, who was bewildered.

"Umm…I don't know what to say. I didn't help you because I expected repayment, so I don't really need you to do that. Especially if you're doing it reluctantly and never thanking me as long as you live… I can't tell whether you're grateful or not…"

"You helped him? You're a real busybody, scarecrow." Challe sounded annoyed.

"Anyway, I couldn't just stand by and let you die. Um, you said your name is Mithril?"

"My name is Mithril Lid Pod. Don't shorten it!"

"Ah, s-sorry. Mithril Lid Pod. In any case, you don't have to repay me, so—"

"Out of the question! Let me do it!"

The fairy's incredible haughtiness made Anne feel suddenly exhausted.

"Maybe it's because I haven't had much contact with fairies up until now…but I thought they were more noble and charming. I was completely wrong, wasn't I? Between you, and Challe, and Cathy…why are you all so stuck-up?"

"Come on, let me return the favor!"

"But I told you, there's really no need."

"No need? Don't be ridiculous! Even if I have to follow you to the depths of hell, I'll make it happen!"

"What's this about hell?! That's so scary! I can't tell whether you're out to pay me back or get revenge! Why are you threatening me?!"

"Just let me repay the favor I owe you. Until I do that, I'm tagging along."

"Fine! Fine, I get it!! All right, I'll take you up on it! Let's see, umm…"

Anne looked around at her surroundings, then clapped her hands loudly.

"Got it! As repayment, would you please oil the axles of my wagon?"

"Don't make light of me! Are you really gonna make me do something so dull as that in return for saving my very life?! You need to think of something way more amazing!!"

"An amazing repayment…like what?"

Anne held her head in her hands.

With a cold expression, Challe asked, "Want me to strangle him to death and shut him up? If you order me to, I'll do it."

Mithril was being very loud, but Challe's tone was so harsh that Anne couldn't tell if he was serious or joking.

When he heard Challe's threat, Mithril launched a ferocious counterattack.

"Why, you!! How dare you say that about a fellow fairy?! Hmph! You must be made of obsidian. Are you looking down on me because I come from a water droplet? Hey, hey, human girl!"

"Anne."

"Anne. This guy under your control is a fairy killer. You need to give him a wallop, just like a fairy hunter would!"

"Wha…? Why are you ordering me around? Who are you?"

"Come on, let's strangle him."

Anne groaned at Challe's strangely forceful proposition.

"Don't say stupid things like that after I went out of my way to rescue you. Anyway, look. You're free, so I want you to go wherever you like and live happily ever after."

"Go where I like?! Are you trying to get rid of me?! Well, I won't go!"

"That's not what I meant, but… I'm just…so tired… I'm going to sleep…"

The conversation with the rambunctious Mithril seemed like it could go on forever without reaching a conclusion.

Anne wearily turned her back on him and got ready for bed, wrapping herself in her blanket.

"Sorry, Challe…I'll make you some sugar candy tomorrow night. By way of apology for the wait, I'll make it something super pretty. If you want to eat candy, don't steal your wing back while I'm asleep, okay?"

Whether or not Challe was actually enticed by the promise of candy, Anne felt pathetic relying on threats like that.

But it was a practical matter. If he reclaimed his wing and disappeared, she would be in real trouble, so there was no way around it.

"I wouldn't worry about that… I doubt you'll be falling asleep anytime soon," Challe grumbled gloomily.

"Hey, you two!! Hey, don't sleep, no sleeping—!!"

Anne covered her ears with her hands, trying to block out Mithril's piercing voice.

"I don't think he's going to let us get any sleep tonight…"

She deeply regretted her own benevolence.

"Hey, hey, hey! Don't you go to sleep, too!! We're supposed to be friends!"

"I don't need any friends as annoying as you."

Challe lay down with a sigh. He was totally fed up with Mithril Lid Pod, who was still bouncing around.

"Wh-wh-what was that? What did you say—?"

"Payback? Are you stupid? She's a human. Have you forgotten the pain when your wing was taken?"

The wings are the most sensitive part of a fairy's body. The pain of having one plucked off is akin to losing a limb.

Being put through that agony is more than enough to make most fairies hate humans.

But Mithril snorted. "What are you talking about? I'll never forget that pain. That's why I'll never say thank you to a human as long as I live. But Anne wasn't the one who took my wing. Anne got it back for me.

Whether human or fairy, good people are good, and bad people are bad, and I'm going to repay favors to any good ones. That's why I'm going to repay Anne! I'm gonna pay-pay-pay her back!"

Mithril seemed to have some unusual ideas regarding the notion of payback, but at any rate, it was clear he was truly grateful to Anne from the bottom of his heart.

Regardless, he was still very noisy.

"Will you shut up?!"

Challe raised his hand, and the moment Mithril jumped into the air, Challe slapped him back down.

Mithril let out a screech as he crashed to the ground. He stared daggers at Challe, then started bouncing around next to Challe's head, even more agitated than before.

"No more violence!! You fairy killer! Killer of your own kind!!"

Fairies who have had one wing removed lose their ability to truly fly. But by flapping the remaining wing and jumping, they can just about reach the height of a human head. Mithril used his wing to help him bounce around Challe, making himself even more of a nuisance.

Striking Mithril had only added to the clamor. Challe realized it would be wiser not to raise his hand against the smaller fairy again.

Anne, who was lying down with her hands over her ears, scowled hard in annoyance.

Anne had apparently saved this fairy, Mithril Lid Pod.

She was so softhearted, it was astounding. She was even soft on Challe.

Anne had served him soup before serving herself. What's more, she had offered to make him sugar candy. She was treating him just like she would another human.

On top of all that, Anne wasn't giving Challe stern orders. Hers were more like requests. He could clearly see she didn't want to damage his wing. She had none of the resolve required to set him to work.

Being ordered around was different than being asked to do things.

So Challe was frankly perplexed. He didn't know whether he should obey her or ignore her.

He resented the idea of obeying her without being forced to do so. But Anne was still in possession of Challe's wing. If she got into any trouble, his wing might also suffer damage.

After some deliberation, he had ultimately driven the bandits away.

By no means had he been following Anne's commands when he did. She was far too lenient for them to even be considered orders.

Challe wondered why Anne was so softhearted. Perhaps because she was lonely? She was a young girl who called out for her mother in her dreams. Of course she would get lonely, traveling all by herself. Perhaps she was unconsciously searching for someone who could alleviate her isolation.

With Mithril clamoring around, Challe didn't think he would have a chance of stealing his wing from Anne that night.

Well, I don't mind.

Challe was hardly being given any commands, which was more comfortable for him anyway. He didn't have to do anything but smile and watch Anne get flustered. She truly was a sweet little girl.

A sudden thought popped into his mind.

The sugar candy the scarecrow makes must be very sweet indeed.

Chapter 3
ATTACK!

Challe sat beside Anne on the driver's seat, looking exhausted. Wedged into the gap between Anne and Challe, curled up into a ball as he slept, was Mithril Lid Pod.

With the rising of the sun, Anne steered the boxy wagon out of the way station.

Mithril had made a fuss throughout the night. Naturally, neither Anne nor Challe had gotten much sleep. She had still been trying to calm Mithril down as they'd departed that morning.

Mithril then had the nerve to sit up on the driver's seat. The sleep-deprived Anne and Challe weren't speaking, and Mithril must have been worn out from staying up all night, because the pleasant swaying of the wagon lulled him into a deep slumber.

Challe looked down at where Mithril was dozing and asked hatefully, "Shall we throw him over the side while he's asleep?"

"That's taking it too far; forget about it. Besides, even if you tossed him out, he'd probably come back. He said he was following me to the depths of hell, after all. He's most likely not going to let us sleep until he does something he considers proper repayment. I don't know what to do… Come to think of it, I don't know what to do about Jonas, either…"

Jonas's wagon was following behind them, as if it were the most natural thing in the world.

After being tossed about on the wagon for a while, Anne looked up and checked the position of the sun.

It was almost time to take a break and have lunch. Anne had noticed a small, clear stream running through the woods that flanked the road. Once they found a clearing, she drove the wagon into it and parked.

Jonas also brought his carriage to gentle stop.

Anne grabbed a bucket and industriously began drawing water from the stream, refilling the cask attached to the side of her wagon.

Jonas watched her for a moment, then seemed to realize that he also needed to replenish his water. He picked up a bucket and walked over to the stream.

Anne had leaned over the side of the stream to scoop up water, and Jonas leaned over in the same manner beside her.

She noticed his presence and turned to face him.

Jonas wore an uncharacteristically serious expression as he stared back at Anne. He then said suddenly, "Anne. Do you understand now? I was worried about you, that's all."

Jonas put his hand into the stream and touched Anne's hand.

This startled her, and she pulled her bucket out of the water. She didn't know how to deal with Jonas when he did things like that. But as always, he was as kind as could be.

"Anne."

When he said her name, a small sigh escaped Anne's lips.

Jonas was a good person. Even his reckless actions were for her sake.

"Very soon, we will have traveled three hundred karons along the Bloody Highway. We've already come one-fourth of the way. At this point, it would be more dangerous for you to turn back and go home alone. It'll be safer if we travel as far as Lewiston together. Let's go together," Anne said.

Hearing that, Jonas burst into a smile.

"So you get it?!"

"In exchange, I need you to understand that we really are in danger out here."

"But you've got a warrior fairy working for you, don't you, Anne? I don't think there's any need to worry."

"Warrior fairies aren't all-powerful. Don't let your faith in Challe make you careless."

"I know that."

Anne didn't sense a shred of nervousness in Jonas's voice as he answered.

She didn't think the young man had spent much time outside Knoxberry

Village. At most, he had probably gone to Redington on occasion to shop or attend festivals. Evidently, a boy like that would be ignorant of the perils the road could hold.

On the other hand, Jonas had been attacked by bandits just the day before. Anne thought he should have shown more concern.

Challe had driven the bandits off much too easily. That had likely given Jonas the incorrect impression that, as long as they were accompanied by a warrior fairy, they had no reason to fret over anything bad happening.

When they finished drawing water, Anne's party ate lunch and then set off again.

On schedule, they arrived at the way station where Anne had decided to spend the third night.

That evening, Anne invited Jonas to eat with her.

As always, she built a small fire.

She spread leather mats out beside the fire and called for Challe, Jonas, and Cathy.

Mithril had already shown up, no summons necessary. He was pacing restlessly around the group, as if observing them.

"Let me introduce you to Jonas and Cathy. This is Challe Fenn Challe. He's a warrior fairy. I purchased him in Redington to serve as my bodyguard. I call him Challe."

"What about a name? You haven't given him one?"

"I just told you his name."

Jonas looked bewildered to be introduced to a fairy. Fairies were like tools, he thought, not the kind of thing that would normally warrant an introduction. The principle of a fairy's owner not giving them a new name was something else he didn't quite understand.

Cathy was giving Challe a curious look, but he turned away, as if he didn't even see her or her master.

Jonas looked Challe over again closely.

"You're really too pretty to be a warrior fairy. What a waste. I bet you could be sold as a pet fairy."

Challe answered coolly, "If you like me, maybe you could buy me from the scarecrow? You're about equally stupid, so I don't care which one of you is in charge of me."

"Challe!"

In a panic, Anne tried to stifle him, but once the words were out of his mouth, there was no way to pretend he hadn't said them.

"S-stupid..."

Clearly, Jonas had never been called stupid by a fairy. Rather than angry, he was dumbfounded.

Anne felt responsible for the insult and began making excuses. "S-sorry, Jonas! Challe's got a sharp tongue; apparently, he didn't sell as a pet fairy. Even as a warrior fairy, I got him at a discount because of it. He's always calling me stupid or moronic or something, so don't take it personally! Challe, don't say things like that to other people besides me. They're not used to it!"

"Hmm. Well...it's not your fault, Anne, so it's fine. More importantly, who is that fairy?"

As if to collect himself, Jonas turned his gaze toward Mithril.

Thinking it was his turn on stage, the little stowaway hopped into the center of the circle.

"Oh, me? My name is Mr. Mithril Lid Pod!! Don't forget the *Mister* when you speak to me!"

"Huh? M-Mister??"

Jonas blinked dramatically. He looked like he didn't grasp Mithril's meaning.

"Why do you both have such attitudes?!" Anne snapped. "Listen, Mithril Lid Pod, I've got a problem with calling you 'Mister.' It clearly doesn't feel right."

In response to Anne's scolding, Mithril hung his head dejectedly. Then, he walked off unsteadily in the direction of Anne's wagon.

As a matter of course, Jonas did not introduce Cathy.

Anne's evening meal consisted of water and a sandwich made of thinly cut slices of dried meat on brown bread. She gave the same to Challe, too.

When she glanced over at Mithril, he was sitting on the roof of the cargo hold of the wagon, melodramatically holding his knees to his chest and drawing circles with his fingertip.

Mithril could be terribly disruptive. He'd made a great nuisance of himself the night before.

But thinking on it more, Anne thought it very admirable of him to be so determined to return a favor. Still, the person he had to repay was a member of the human race he so despised. Maybe that was why he was so prone to making such bizarre pronouncements.

He's really cute when he isn't talking. He's got those big round eyes and everything.

Anne split her own sandwich in two and beckoned Mithril over.

"Come here, Mithril. You can have this."

Mithril's face burst into a bright smile, and he went bounding over and snatched the sandwich from Anne's hand.

Then with a serious face, he commented, "I am Mithril Lid Pod. Don't abbreviate it!"

"Of course. I'm sorry. Mithril Lid Pod."

Anne had considered splitting her dinner with Jonas, too, but he'd insisted he had his own food and retrieved it from his wagon.

Jonas's meal struck Anne as unbelievably luxurious.

He had grape wine. Apple juice. White-bread sandwiches filled with pear jam. A slice of meat pie. His mother had obviously spared no expense in provisioning his journey. It was a picnic fit for the young master.

Once Anne saw his spread, she was convinced Jonas had set off with his parents' consent.

Assembling such a variety of foods was a feat only the mistress of the house could perform. Jonas's parents had supplied the wagon and the food and had hired some bodyguards while they were at it. They had arranged everything for him. Of that, Anne had no doubt.

But why had the Anders supported their son's reckless behavior? That part didn't make sense.

"If you've got feasts like this with you, I guess you don't need my soup or anything, huh?" Anne grumbled mindlessly.

In response, Cathy, who was pouring wine into Jonas's cup, chuckled. "Of course not."

Jonas glared at Cathy.

"Be quiet, Cathy. I forbid you to speak to Anne in such a rude tone."

Startled, the servant fairy's demeanor shifted. She was flustered and tried to mend her error.

"Ah, forgive me, Master Jonas. I was just—"

"Disappear."

Cathy hung her head. Colors began fading from her body, starting from the tips of her toes, and she quickly became transparent. In the end, her whole body disappeared. Only the wine bottle she was holding remained visible, floating lightly in the air.

Fairies have unique abilities. Cathy's ability seemed to be invisibility.

"Sorry about that, Anne," Jonas said apologetically. "My servant fairy sometimes shows poor manners. Your soup was delicious, truly. I was happy to receive it."

Jonas's behavior was probably what was expected of a young gentleman, but Anne still felt bad for Cathy. Just before disappearing, she'd looked absolutely miserable.

The following morning, the two wagons set out again.

Mithril sat happily between Challe and Anne. He was in a good mood, chattering on and on.

"Anne. If there's something I can do to repay my debt to you, don't hold back—tell me. But don't ask me to do odd jobs. Let me do something more impressive as repayment."

"An impressive repayment, huh? I've been thinking it might be best to come up with something that uses your special ability, if possible. What kind of powers do you have, Mithril Lid Pod?"

Hearing this inquiry, Mithril threw out his chest as if he'd been waiting for his cue.

"Oh, my powers? You'll be surprised to hear! Listen carefully. I come from the waters of Loess Lake, a huge lake in the northernmost part of the Kingdom of Highland! …A drop of lake water stuck to a leaf, and I was born from that droplet."

"You were born from a drop of water? Are all fairies born that way?"

Anne cocked her head, and Mithril wagged his index finger chidingly.

"You don't know a thing, do you, Anne? Fairies are born from all sorts of things. Berries and nuts, water droplets and morning dew, stones and gems. When the energy of an object condenses enough, a fairy is born. But in order for that to happen, the gaze of a living creature is required.

It can be another fairy, a human, a beast, or a bird. Even a fish or a bug will do. The energy takes on a form as the object is being observed, and that form becomes a fairy. A fairy's life span is approximately the same as the object from which it originated."

"So Mithril Lid Pod was born from a water droplet. What were you born from, Challe?"

Challe just glanced over at Anne and didn't answer.

Mithril replied instead.

"Judging from his appearance, I'd say that guy came from a piece of obsidian. Stone fairies have the power to make sharp objects. Since I was born from a water droplet, I can control water. That's my power."

"Control water?! That's incredible! Show me!"

"Sure!"

Mithril cupped both hands in front of his chest.

He stared hard into his little palms, and water bubbled up to fill the hollow.

Mithril formed the water into a ball just like he was working a piece of clay, and he tossed it gently up into the air. It burst when it hit the back of Anne's hand. It was only a small splash, but she could feel the coolness of the lake water.

"Amazing! If you can control water, then if we're ever caught in a flash flood, you can change the course of the water, right?!"

"Don't talk about such dreadful things. Who could possibly do that?"

"So what can you do?"

"I just showed you!"

"Huh...... That's all?"

"Yes, but...what? Got something to say?"

Anne's shoulders drooped in disappointment. It seemed like Mithril's powers didn't amount to much.

"You'll be useful if we ever need to give water to a baby bird," Challe remarked, his voice thick with sarcasm.

"Grr, shut up, you!! What does that even mean? Are you making fun of me? I won't let you talk to me like that! And while I'm at it, Challe Fenn Challe, you ought to treat Anne better, too! You're so rude!"

"You're ruder than I am," Challe retorted coolly.

"What's rude about me?"

"Everything."

"What did you say?!"

Giving the two quarreling fairies a sidelong look, Anne declared, "It's all right, there's no need to fight about it. You're both equally rude."

Anne steadily scooched away from them.

If they managed to make it to the way station where Anne had decided they would spend the fourth night of their journey that evening, they would have traveled four hundred karons down the Bloody Highway. They would be one-third of the way to their destination.

The sun gradually sank in the sky, painting the edges of the distant mountains a bright orange.

Anne was wondering whether they might reach the next way station without issue when the rays of sunlight, which had been shining on the back of the wagon as if pushing it onward, suddenly grew dim.

Challe looked up at the sky and frowned. Mithril looked up as well, following Challe's lead, and his whole expression changed.

"Hey, Challe Fenn Challe. That's..."

Anne tilted her head quizzically when she heard Mithril's serious tone.

"What? What's wrong?"

That same moment, Jonas pulled his wagon up alongside Anne's so that his driver's seat was even with hers.

"Hey, Anne. Anne! Look up."

When she saw Jonas's frightened expression, Anne finally realized that something strange was going on.

Following Jonas's finger, she looked high up into the sky.

Anne was startled. The heavens were black.

She had assumed it had gotten cloudy, that the light from the sun had just been obstructed.

But it wasn't clouds that had blocked the light.

It was a flock of wasteland crows, several hundred strong. The huge, black birds had gathered and been flying behind them, following them without uttering a single cry.

"This is...an attack..."

Anne had heard rumors about the wasteland crows.

The crows are scavengers that usually feed on carrion. But whenever there isn't enough to feed them, they swarm and descend on living things, killing them for food.

It is said that when they strike, their target is beyond hope.

Using their sharp beaks, they first aim for the eyes of their prey. The crows pin their victims down, then tear off pieces of flesh. Hiding inside a wagon is pointless. The crows are intelligent. They patiently cling to the boards of the roof of the cargo hold and peck holes in them until they break through.

Anne trembled in fear at the sight of the flock of pitch-black birds filling the sky.

She knew that if they were attacked, they were as good as dead. Anne and her group couldn't repel them.

Anne looked over at Challe. This time, it was absolutely necessary to order him to act. Her life and everyone else's were in danger. She had to do it. *If you don't want your wing destroyed, protect us from the wasteland crows.* But—

"Challe, please."

Anne said it without thinking. Challe's eyes flashed when he heard the word *please*. Without him saying a thing, Anne felt as if he had scolded her: *Are you still trying to pretend we're friends?*

She weathered the rebuke and steadied herself.

"Challe. I command you. Protect us from the wasteland crows. I've got your wing in my hand. You know what that means, right?"

She issued the order, but it didn't feel right.

Truthfully, Anne did not want to do anything cruel like crush Challe's wing. But if the warrior fairy saw through her act, he might not follow her orders.

Sure enough, Challe narrowed his eyes in a look of amusement.

Anne didn't know what she would do if he refused. There would likely be nothing for it except to remove the wing from where she kept it concealed near her chest and act like she was going to tear it up.

But Challe nodded. He then ordered, "Park the wagons."

With those few words, he jumped down from the driver's seat. In a panic, Anne pulled her wagon to a stop and looked back at him. As the sword made from condensed light appeared in his hand, he said bluntly over his shoulder, "Hide yourselves in the cargo hold."

He obeyed me? Why?

The crows began their descent toward the now-stationary group.

"Anne!"

Jonas stopped his carriage as well and looked up at the sky with a pale face.

"Jonas, get in your cargo hold! Hurry!"

Hearing that, Jonas quickly took refuge.

"This is it! My chance to repay you! I will also help drive away the birds!"

Mithril rubbed his hands together and stood, rolling up his sleeves with surprising determination.

Anne went pale, too.

"No way, nuh-uh! Not on your life! Come here!"

"Whaddaya mean, 'no way'?! Don't complain about me paying back a favor… Ahhh!"

Anne grabbed the grumbling Mithril by the collar, jumped down from the driver's seat, and leaped into the back of her wagon.

"Don't go out there. If you die trying to repay me, then there was no point in saving you."

Anne sat on the floor of the cargo hold, embracing Mithril tightly.

"But I… My debt… Repay…"

Mithril's voice trailed off as Anne hugged him, and his cheeks gradually reddened. At last, he was quiet.

Anne listened to the noises happening outside.

The crows were silent before, but now they were cawing in unison, like a battle cry.

Anne instinctively covered her ears with both hands as she was assailed by a storm of sound crashing down on her from above.

With great terrible *thumps*, the crows hurled themselves at the wagon, which rattled and shook.

It was all Anne could do to stifle her screams.

Protect us…Challe!

The wagon swayed violently. The horse was panicking and struggling.

The cries of the wasteland crows seemed to envelop the whole vehicle.

Anne couldn't keep her body from quaking. She curled up into a ball, paralyzed.

As she huddled there, Mithril's tiny hand gently touched her face.

"Don't be scared, Anne. We'll be all right. Challe Fenn Challe comes from obsidian. He's not like me. He can't get hurt, and he can't be broken. He's exceptionally strong, even compared with other fairies."

After quite a long time, the crow's attacks on the wagon finally abated. The rasping caws diminished. Bit by bit, it grew quiet outside.

Perfect stillness returned. Anne and Mithril looked at each other.

"Is it over?"

"Um…I don't know."

Anne lifted her head, placed Mithril on the floor, and rose. She cautiously opened the door.

As soon as she did, something black dropped down right in front of her with a *thud*.

"Ah!!"

She fell on her backside and scooted away.

The carcass of a wasteland crow had slipped off the roof and landed on the wagon steps. Once she realized what it was, Anne looked up.

Through the open door, she could see a pitch-black highway.

The road was buried in crow corpses, blanketed in black feathers.

Standing atop the carpet of black feathers was Challe, his white cheeks covered in splashes of blood.

"…Challe."

When she called his name, the warrior fairy turned to look at Anne.

His eyes were sharp, as they always were, yet somehow vacant. He truly looked like a blade honed from obsidian.

Challe swung the sword in his hand and made it vanish, then casually wiped the blood off his cheeks. He slowly walked over the black carpet of feathers toward Anne.

When he saw her sitting on the floor, he chuckled dismissively.

"Weak in the knees?"

"N-no, I'm not!"

Anne stubbornly denied it, trying to rise, but there was no strength in her legs, and she stumbled.

She nearly tumbled off the wagon, and Challe caught her in his arms.

The moment he did, a breeze fluttered Challe's wing, which gently

brushed against Anne's cheek. The sensation of the wing, softer than silk, sent a sweet shiver up her spine.

Anne looked up and saw black eyes looking back at her. Without meaning to, she gazed into them deeply.

The darkness she found there seemed like it could swallow her. *How beautiful he is*, she thought again. The color and luster of those eyes were enough to make her melt under their gaze.

"What is it, scarecrow? Hoping for something more?"

Challe whispered the mean-spirited question in a sensual voice, and Anne immediately lost her cool.

"Get real!!"

In a panic, she pushed herself away from him and turned her back.

"Anyway, th-thank you for saving us."

Challe thought it best if she didn't realize that she was blushing.

"There are so many. If they had attacked us, we definitely would have been dead meat."

Picking up the hem of her dress to step over the corpses of the wasteland crows, Anne made her way to her driver's seat. Jonas also got down from his wagon's cargo hold and walked next to Anne.

"He really saved us, huh? Anne, thank goodness you have Challe under your control."

Anne looked back at Challe with a troubled expression on her face.

"Uh...yeah, I guess so."

Anne started walking again, and Challe smiled wryly as he watched her go.

Anne had tried her very best to act tough so she could make Challe follow her orders.

However, her commands carried none of the cruelty of a true master. It was clear to Challe that, although she might threaten to crush his wing, she was incapable of carrying out that threat.

Even so, Challe had protected Anne and the others. He didn't do it because he was following orders. If Anne had been pecked to death by the crows, his wing, which was in her possession, would also have been in danger.

That was the only reason he had defended Anne.

The girl had to know how tenuous her control over him was and that he saw right through her bravado. She also suspected that it was not her command that had driven Challe to action.

It seemed like her intuition in that regard was good.

You're holding my wing. Pull yourself together, scarecrow.

Anne was less of a master, and more like a burden. She was holding on to his wing and wouldn't let it go, so he couldn't treat her roughly. Neither could he leave her side.

From Challe's perspective, it was like he was walking around with a living treasure box that had lost its key and couldn't be opened.

Why is such a hopeless girl traveling all by herself?

He found it quite curious indeed.

Anne comforted the frightened horse and kept her hand on the bit to guide it slowly through the carcasses of the wasteland crows. The number of bodies was immense. Although she knew that if Challe hadn't killed them, she and her party would have been in mortal danger, actually feeling how many lives had been extinguished underfoot put Anne in a somber mood.

Some of those crows probably left chicks behind in their nests…

But assuming that such violence was necessary for Anne to survive her journey, she would have to find some way to reconcile her feelings toward similar incidents moving forward.

Emma had always shielded Anne's eyes and protected her from bad and scary things, but she wasn't around anymore.

It wasn't long before the horse regained its composure, and the wagon was able to resume its normal pace.

Anne was finally able to settle back in the driver's seat.

However, she looked up and frowned.

"This is bad."

The sun had sunk halfway behind the mountains. The eastern sky was already beginning to turn a dark indigo.

They had lost a lot of time fending off the wasteland crows.

As things stood, it would be difficult for them to make it to a way station before the sun set completely.

"It's just one thing after another."

"What will you do? Spend the night in the wagons?" Challe asked.

Sitting next to Anne, Challe seemed to have realized the dilemma already.

"If it comes to that, I'll have to ask you to stay up and keep watch, and I can't put that burden on you after you just drove away the wasteland crows for us..."

"Leave it to me! I'll take the night watch! This time, it's my chance to shine!" Mithril chimed in from between Anne and Challe, raising his hands enthusiastically in the air.

She smiled wryly.

"If there's nothing more we can do, I'll take you up on that, but let's hold off for the moment."

Anne extracted a map from the bottom of the cargo hold and traced her finger along the highway drawn on it.

The way station where she had planned to spend the fourth night was still quite a trek away. Much closer than the way station, though, just a little farther ahead from where Anne and her party were at the moment, something else was marked on the map.

It was labeled *Doctor's Inn*.

Jonas pulled his wagon up alongside Anne's and peered at the horizon uneasily.

"Anne, it's going to be dark soon. I don't suppose there's anything we can do but run for the way station?"

"The wild beasts will come out as soon as the sun goes down. It's dangerous to travel after dark. We've got to take refuge somewhere safe before that happens. If we go a little farther, there's a Doctor's Inn. Let's try to stay there. If we make it and find that it's closed, well, at least we tried. It's that, accept the risks and try to make a run for the way station, or park the wagons by the side of the road and spend the night in the cargo holds. Which would you prefer?"

Anne quickly folded the map as she informed him of their options.

Jonas cocked his head. "What's a Doctor's Inn?"

"As the name suggests, it's a house belonging to a doctor. Doctors who practice in remote areas offer lodgings for travelers. Even bandits need medical assistance sometimes, right? So they almost never attack these inns, and as a result, doctors' houses are safe havens. But sometimes, a doctor might die or move away, and the house goes with them. It's best not to really rely on them during a journey, but…we'll have to hope it's still there. Anyway, let's hurry!"

Anne whipped the horse. To be expected, Jonas looked apprehensive and set his wagon in motion.

The pitiless sun was sinking before their eyes.

The dark sky emerging in the east filled Anne with fear.

Anne whipped the horse again, urging it to go faster. But Anne's horse was old. She didn't want to handle it too roughly.

Emma would have been able to get a precise read on the horse's fatigue by listening to its breathing and make it run just at its limit. Anne wasn't that skilled yet.

Her impatience grew stronger in the face of the approaching darkness.

"We need to go faster…but I guess there's no way? What should we do? If Mama were here, she would do everything right," she mumbled absently, staring straight ahead.

Challe glanced over at her.

"That mother of yours, where is she now?"

The question sent a shock of pain through Anne's heart. She forced a smile in an attempt to hold the pain at bay.

Then she said, as cheerfully as possible, "I guess I never told you that Mama died."

A small glimpse of surprise appeared on Challe's otherwise emotionless face.

"My mother was a Silver Sugar Master. She died a few weeks ago. Mama and I traveled constantly, all around the country, so I don't really have a place to call home. And I don't have any relatives, aside from Mama. After she died, I thought about what I should do with my life and decided to become a Silver Sugar Master, too. To achieve that, I need to enter the Royal Candy Fair in Lewiston and win. I want to become a Silver Sugar Master this year no matter what. Do you know why?"

Challe shrugged. Of course he didn't.

Anne continued. To keep herself from thinking about unnecessary things, she kept her gaze locked on the approaching darkness, thinking only about hurrying forward as she spoke.

"In winter, we have Pure Soul Day, right? The holiday when we say good-bye to all the people who passed that year. When that holiday comes around, I want to make an amazing sugar candy with my own hands as a Silver Sugar Master and send Mama's soul off to heaven. The best candy in the country, made by my own two hands! If I do that, Mama will be able to rest in peace, don't you think? It's a great idea, right?"

Anne rattled on, babbling in a cheerful voice without stopping. She kept talking because she felt that, if she stopped, something in her chest would burst.

The reason she wanted to make it in time for the Royal Candy Fair.

The reason she was so intent on becoming a Silver Sugar Master that year.

It was all to send her mother off to heaven with the best sugar candy, made with her own skills that had been recognized as the very best.

That was her sole motivation.

Even Anne knew it was sentimental.

But she was desperate to do it. It was the only thing she desired.

Anne felt like there was something within reach, something she could do for Emma. She feared that if she stopped moving toward that goal, the ground beneath her feet might crumble, bit by bit, sending her plummeting into bottomless darkness.

Challe stared intently at Anne, as if searching for something. Apparently born from obsidian, he had eyes that were certainly beautiful and strong like volcanic glass.

Anne refused to meet Challe's gaze, afraid that those eyes of his would see straight through to her heart.

"If fairies are born from objects, that must mean you all come into this world alone, right? That might be for the best."

Just for a moment, Anne's urgency to hurry forward receded into the background. She almost thought she could hear the sound of a dry, rustling wind blowing through her chest.

"If you have a mother or a family, it's so hard when they pass away. It feels like losing a piece of your heart. If you never have anyone to begin with, you never have to know how it feels to lose them," Anne murmured.

Challe responded quietly, "Even though we're born alone, that doesn't mean we don't know the pain of separation. Neither does it mean fairies can't understand how it feels when someone important to you leaves."

That was all Challe said before sinking back into silence.

Challe had feelings inside that were quite similar to Anne's. His silence convinced her of that.

But that stillness of his was unbearable.

Anne feared that if she said any more, the emotions she had bottled up would overflow.

She was desperate to keep back that great, interminable loneliness. She was sure it dwelled within Challe as well. If she touched on it, her loneliness would immediately overflow and crush her.

Anne kept her eyes fixed forward, only forward.

So that means she's got no mother?

Challe scrutinized Anne's face as she stubbornly stared straight ahead. He thought he understood now. It was clear the girl had been unconsciously seeking a friend to ease the pain of her loneliness.

She's lonesome. This skinny little fifteen-year-old girl is all alone. She's basically helpless. How deep her isolation must be.

An overwhelming loneliness that permeated the body like an abyss. Challe was familiar with the feeling.

He knew Anne probably expected it to vanish once she entered the Royal Candy Fair and became a Silver Sugar Master.

Of course, if she failed to achieve the goal she'd set for herself, she might have a total breakdown.

Challe figured it would probably be the latter.

If those are the options, I hope she can do it.

He recalled the pain from when his wing had been torn off and everything that happened afterward.

He remembered the separation that was even more agonizing than the loss of his wing.

Liz…

Back then, Challe had done the same thing, running toward some barely attainable goal just to keep himself moving.

As long as he kept his eyes on the prize, he didn't have to think or feel.

During that time, he hadn't been particularly happy, but he hadn't been unhappy, either.

If the alternative was a breakdown, he would rather let Anne chase her dream. Even if she was a human, he felt he understood what she was going through.

Mithril was also staring at Anne quietly, looking worried.

Just then, Anne's tense face suddenly brightened.

"Ah! Look—lights!"

The whole sky was steeped in indigo. Off to the right side of the dark highway ahead, tucked into the foothills of the mountains, a compact house appeared on the horizon, surrounded by a high stone wall. It was the Doctor's Inn.

The wall, built of stones of uneven shapes and sizes, had only a single gate with a pair of thick wooden double doors.

Beyond the gate, inside the safety of the stone barrier, they could see a building with a wooden roof. Warm light shone out through the windows.

The heavy doors of the gate were just starting to close.

"Wait!" Anne shouted.

Chapter 4

AN EVENING AT THE DOCTOR'S INN

The person who was about to close the gate was a middle-aged man. He was unsteady on his feet, with a shaggy beard and unkempt, graying hair. But Anne could sense intelligence in his face.

"Wait, wait, please! I beg you!"

When he noticed Anne's and Jonas's wagons rushing toward him, the man left the doors half-open and waited for them.

Anne brought her wagon to a stop when they reached the gate, and she got down from the driver's seat.

She was impatient but didn't forget to show proper respect.

"I'm sorry to bother you after dark like this. Are you the doctor who lives here?"

When he heard her question, the man nodded.

"That's right," he said.

"We're travelers. We were planning to stay at the way station down the road tonight, but we were attacked by wasteland crows and got delayed. There's no way we'll make it there. Please, would you let us stay here just for tonight?"

Even though Doctor's Inns were well-known, they were still private residences. The doctor could choose to turn away travelers.

Anne wanted to win the man's sympathy.

The doctor peered through the dim light to study Anne's carriage.

"It sure looks like you got attacked by crows, doesn't it? There are plenty of marks on the sides of your wagon where they struck it. Good thing you managed to get away safely."

Anne looked back at Challe, who was still sitting.

"It's because he was with us. He's a warrior fairy."

The doctor followed her gaze and looked at Challe. "What a beautiful fairy," he remarked. "You don't see many like this very often. He's a warrior fairy, you say? Not a pet?"

The doctor shuffled up to the driver's seat of the wagon and stared at Challe. He stood still, gazing in fascination at the fairy.

Night had settled over the land, and they could hear the howls of wolves.

Anne was growing tired of waiting but did her best to endure it.

However—

"Are you going to stare at me all night, shaggy?"

Challe sounded fed up.

Anne went pale and nearly screamed at him.

Hyaaah—!! Challe—! How could you—?!!

She felt a rush of cold sweat.

Sure enough, the doctor's hair and beard were the shaggiest she had ever seen. Challe was right; the man was shaggy.

But it would be a disaster if he made the doctor angry.

As if he had awoken from a dream, the doctor blinked several times. Then, he smiled bashfully and turned back toward Anne.

"Ah, sorry, sorry. When you live in a place like this, you don't often get to appreciate genuine beauty. Anyway, you seem to have had quite a difficult time. Please feel free to stay. The charge is sixty bayn per person. If that's all right, you can pull both wagons inside the walls."

"Th-thank you!"

Anne wiped away her cold sweat and hung her head low with relief.

When they got the wagons through the gate, they saw that there was already another guest's conveyance stowed inside.

Anne could see immediately that the lacquer on their carriage was high-quality work. It was old, but solidly constructed.

Jonas, who had parked nearby, came up beside Anne and said quietly, "Look, Anne. This carriage must belong to someone of high social standing. Someone of real importance, you know? That makes me nervous."

"We've got to be on our best behavior, then. Especially Challe—I need him to be more careful about what he says..."

As they were heading toward the door to the house, Anne glared at Challe, who was walking beside her.

"Challe. I thought my heart was going to stop earlier when you called that man 'shaggy.'"

Mithril, who was bouncing along behind Anne, chimed in to criticize the larger fairy.

"That's right, that's right! That guy wasn't *shaggy*; we oughta call him *rickety* instead!"

"Exactly, he was *rickety*, not *shaggy*… Wait, wrooong!!"

Anne shouted at the pair.

"You can't call him 'shaggy' or 'rickety'! What will we do if you make him angry? We'll get kicked out of here!"

Challe answered calmly, "I doubt this particular human would get angry over something so insignificant. I can tell just by looking at him. I'm quite confident about this, since I called all sorts of humans many horrible names back in the fairy marketplace."

"We don't need your strange sense of confidence! In any case, please stop calling him names!"

"It's been my habit for many years, so I'm not sure I can make any promises," Challe said flatly.

Anne slumped her shoulders in defeat.

There was nothing she could do but humble herself and apologize the best she could if her companion angered someone.

Anne opened the door and stepped inside the house.

Just inside was a spacious room with no partitions.

Along one wall was a medicine cabinet and a wooden bed that looked like it was used for treatment. On the opposite wall were three sets of tables and chairs of various materials and designs. It looked like the doctor's infirmary was also the dining room.

The other guests were nowhere to be seen. Anne figured they were probably relaxing in their assigned rooms.

The doctor led Anne and the others to a door in the back of the hall.

Behind it was a corridor running perpendicular to the doorway. At one end of the hallway was a room that looked like a kitchen, while the one on the other end looked like a bathroom.

There were three additional doors on both sides of the hallway, which appeared to be rooms meant for guests.

Anne and Jonas were each given their own room.

There were two beds, and a tidy little curtain hanging over a small window. The space was modest but comfortable.

"Once you put your bags down and rest a bit, come to the dining room. I can serve you a simple soup," the doctor said as he left.

Of course, they didn't have any luggage. Anne was more concerned with her grumbling stomach. Jonas seemed similarly afflicted, as he came into Anne's room complaining of hunger.

Before long, Anne and the others nonchalantly poked their heads into the dining room.

The doctor had set a large pot on one of the tables and was ladling soup into earthenware bowls.

At a different table, two young men were seated. They were facing each other, playing cards.

Jonas whispered to Anne, "Those must be the other guests. Though, they don't look all that important."

One of the men was tall and solidly built. His unkempt brown hair was carelessly arranged, and the shirt, pants, and jacket he was wearing weren't extravagant, though they looked well fitted. However, there were flickers of something wild in his brown eyes that couldn't be concealed, even by smartly tailored clothes.

The other man had a strange appearance. He had a lean, muscular body and tanned skin. His hair was pure white and his eyes gray. He gave the impression of a graceful, feline predator. He was probably from another country. He was dressed in a leather vest and pants, and sitting beside him was a gently curved sword.

Someone important traveling incognito and his bodyguard. That was Anne's guess.

"Oh, here you are. Come this way, the soup's ready," the doctor called out when he noticed Anne's party.

At the sound of the their host's voice, the two young men turned toward the door through which Anne and the others were poking their heads.

"Come and sit here. I don't know how good it is, but we've got plenty to go around. You can eat lots."

"Thank you so much," Anne answered amiably, and they all entered the dining room.

Anne and Jonas took a seat at the table where the doctor had placed the large pot. Once they were seated, Anne noticed that Challe, Mithril, and Cathy were standing far from the table.

"What's wrong, you three? Hurry up and sit down."

Anne called them over. When she did, the doctor and the other guests looked at her with surprise.

"Huh? What?"

Anne recoiled under their gazes, and Jonas whispered, "Anne, you know it's not normal to eat meals with your fairies, right?!"

"But I do it..."

"It's not how things are normally done! This may be an inn, but we're still guests here, right? If you say that kind of thing in a public place, people will think you don't know social etiquette."

Jonas made it clear that Anne had done something that missed the mark as far as so-called social etiquette was concerned. But at the same time, she was angry. She didn't see any reason to demean fairies like that.

"I don't need to know that kind of etiquette. I don't care. Listen, I want to eat with Challe and the others."

Anne looked the doctor in the face.

"We've been eating together this whole journey. I want to continue doing that. If we can't, then I just won't eat at all."

"I see. I don't mind personally, but look, I've got other guests right now, too..."

Suddenly, a loud laugh rang out, drowning out the doctor's mumbling.

"It's no problem!! I don't care, either!"

The laugh came from the man with brown hair. As he chortled, he waved one big hand in Anne's direction.

"Hey, sweetheart, what's your name?"

"Anne. Anne Halford."

"I'm Hugh. Don't worry about it, Anne. Tell your fairies to have a seat."

"Thank you."

Hugh's informal manner and cheerful smile softened the atmosphere.

The fairies looked baffled, unsure of what they should do. Anne invited them to her table.

As she and the others began eating their soup, the young man who had called himself Hugh gathered up the playing cards. He then leaned over from the adjacent table and spoke to Anne.

"Where are you kids from? And where are you headed, traveling down a highway like this?"

"He's—Jonas is from Knoxberry Village. I've never had a permanent place to live ever since I was born, so I can't tell you where I'm from. We're going to Lewiston."

At that point, Jonas puffed up with pride and said somewhat boastfully, "We're going to enter the Royal Candy Fair in Lewiston! We're both candy crafters."

"Ha! You're candy crafters? But you're really traveling in luxury for a couple of ordinary candy crafters. You've got two servant fairies, plus one pet fairy, huh?"

Hugh rose with a grin. He stood beside Challe and peered deliberately at his face.

"Hmm? This one looks expensive. Who owns this pretty pet?"

Challe had his hand on his soup bowl, quietly eating. Just for a second, his sharp eyes glanced over at Hugh, but thankfully, he didn't say anything.

"I bought Challe. But he's not a pet fairy; he's a warrior fairy. He's my bodyguard."

"A warrior fairy? You're pulling my leg. You don't have to be embarrassed about it. It's only natural for a girl your age to want to take a walk with a pretty fairy like him. Did you fall in love with him, Anne? Is that why you bought him?"

Anne could tell he was making fun of her. She flared up with embarrassment.

"It's not like that!"

"Don't get all bashful now. I can tell; you don't have to lie like that."

"I'm not lying!" Anne shouted in spite of herself.

Hugh looked amused, and his eyes flashed.

"All right then, how about you prove it?"

Hugh glanced over at the young man accompanying him and took one step back.

The other traveler, who so far had been quiet enough that he'd faded into the background, reacted to Hugh's signal.

Suddenly, he grabbed the sword sitting beside him and unsheathed it in a single motion, kicking his chair away. He looked like a beast on the prowl readying itself to pounce. The blade streaked through the air toward Challe.

"Challe!"

Faster than Anne could shout his name, the warrior fairy leaped to his feet and jumped out of the way.

Before the second attack reached him, his silver sword appeared in his hand.

The man's weapon swung down at full strength, and Challe's caught the blow.

The blades collided, and the force of the impact sent a ripple through the air.

"Not bad," the young man with the tan skin muttered, expressionless.

Challe smiled and whispered to his opponent, "You want to die?"

"Afraid I'm not that messed up."

The sound of their swords grinding against each other echoed through the room. Their power was well matched, and neither could advance.

"I see. He really is a warrior fairy," Hugh said with a smile, sounding amazed. "That's enough, Salim. Put away your sword."

The man whom Hugh had called Salim readily withdrew his blade.

Challe shrugged, dropped his fighting stance, and let his sword disappear.

Once Anne came to her senses, she rose without thinking and grabbed Hugh by the collar.

"What do you think you're doing, you idiot?!" she demanded. "If you hurt my companion, I'll make you pay!"

"Sorry, sorry, don't get so upset. I just couldn't believe that such a pretty fairy could really be a warrior. I wanted to test him, that's all," Hugh said without a hint of remorse.

"You think that excuses what you did?!"

"Come on, I'm apologizing here. To make it up to you, I'll pay the lodging fee for the lot of you."

"You can't weasel your way out of… Wait… Huh? The lodging fee? …Really?"

The hand holding Hugh's collar slackened.

The cost of Emma's medical treatments over the past half a year had been considerable. Anne had also been unable to earn much money during that time. She had burned through all their savings and used what little she had left to purchase Challe.

The lodging fees would bankrupt her.

Consequently, Anne was incredibly grateful to hear Hugh's offer.

"One, two, three…five people, at sixty bayn a head—that comes to three cress, yeah?" Hugh said. "That's quite a sum. A bit too expensive for a simple apology."

"What do you mean? It was your suggestion, wasn't it?!"

"You got me there. But I feel like I'm losing out a little. I know, you said you two are candy crafters, right? Make me one piece of candy each. If you do that, I'll pay the lodging fees for all five of you."

"Huh?!"

"Something roughly palm-sized will do. At most, two candies of that size would cost about ten bayn, right? You'll be spending ten bayn to earn three cress—not a bad return, is it?"

Anne had a feeling that Hugh was toying with them.

But the idea of not having to pay the lodging fee was an attractive one.

She turned and looked at Jonas. Jonas shrugged.

"I've got no objections, Anne."

For some reason, Jonas looked delighted.

Anne turned back toward Hugh and said with a huff, "All right, fine. We'll make you candy. And in exchange, you'd better pay up!"

"If you like, I could take a knee and swear an oath."

"I don't need it. Just be patient. Once we're finished eating, we'll make your candy."

When they had finished their meal, Anne and Jonas went together to retrieve the silver sugar from Anne's wagon.

Inside the cargo hold of the wagon, lined up along one of the walls, were five silver sugar barrels.

One was empty. Another was about two-thirds full of silver sugar. The remaining three were tightly packed, all the way up to the rims.

Entrants in the Royal Candy Fair in Lewiston present a single work of candy art for the festival.

Along with these, they must also submit three barrels of silver sugar.

This is because they are judged not only by the quality of their crafting but also by their skill at stabilizing and refining fine-quality silver sugar.

Refining silver sugar from sugar apples had been Anne's job since she was ten years old.

"We can't use these three barrels, but even after I make my entry for the candy fair out of the two-thirds-full barrel, I'll have plenty left over. We could make ten palm-sized candies, and I'd still have more than enough," Anne mumbled as she opened the lid on the barrel.

She scooped some silver sugar into a stone vessel and handed it to Jonas. She filled one more for herself, then exited the wagon.

"This is kind of exciting, huh?" Jonas chirped happily as they headed back to the house.

Anne was doubtful. "Why? I've got a feeling that this guy is making fun of us."

"Even so, don't you feel proud to show off your skills in front of other people?"

"I guess so."

"I sure do. I've got confidence in my skills. Actually, keep this between us, but there's a very good chance I'm going to get an endorsement to become the future maestro of the Radcliffe Workshop! The current maestro there saw some of my work… He's a distant relative of mine, but apparently, he took a liking to me. Of course, in order to become maestro, I first have to become a Silver Sugar Master."

There are three large factions of candy crafters.

The Mercury Workshop.

The Paige Workshop.

And the Radcliffe Workshop.

If a crafter isn't affiliated with one of these factions, they may face difficulty obtaining sugar apples, the raw material that goes into making silver sugar. They might also have a hard time selling the candy they create.

That is why the majority of candy crafters are affiliated with one of the three factions.

Of course, the rival factions are in constant competition.

Anne's mother, Emma, did not join any of them. She'd claimed she didn't care for the factions' way of doing things. She had struggled to obtain sugar apples and to sell her sugar candies.

Whenever Anne heard Jonas boasting, it made her realize that he lived in a different world, with a totally different set of values than her.

However, their aspiration to become Silver Sugar Masters seemed the same, though it might have been the only thing they shared in common.

"So you want to become a Silver Sugar Master too, huh, Jonas? Why don't you enter this year's Royal Candy Fair?"

"Well, I…I've entered twice, last year and the year before that, but I haven't been able to become a Silver Sugar Master yet. I'm sitting out this year. I'm going to polish my skills a little more and go for it next year! For the sake of my future, I need to become a Silver Sugar Master. If I don't, I can never lead the Radcliffe Workshop. And I can never work up to be a Silver Sugar Viscount."

Anne's eyebrows rose in surprise when she heard those words.

"Jonas, you want to become Viscount?"

The Silver Sugar Viscount is an individual chosen from among all the Silver Sugar Masters to work exclusively for the royal household.

The title is granted to that Silver Sugar Master and only them. It cannot be passed down through their bloodline.

All the candy-crafter factions must follow the orders of the Silver Sugar Viscount. Failing to do so is considered the same as disobeying a royal edict.

Becoming Viscount is a peak achievement for any candy crafter.

"I sure do! Actually, I know I'm going to make Viscount. I mean, the son of commoners becoming a noble? There's no greater dream, is there? So, Anne—"

Suddenly, Jonas stopped walking. Anne stopped, too.

"So won't you please marry me? I'm going to become a Silver Sugar Master and then Silver Sugar Viscount. I can promise you a happy life."

The moon poked its face out from between two clouds. Anne could see Jonas's expression clearly.

She should have been happy to hear those words, but she tried to imagine leading a happy life with the boy in front of her. The vision evaded her.

Even looking at Jonas's handsome face and hearing his proposal didn't stir her heart.

Rather than Jonas…

Suddenly, an image of Challe floated up in Anne's mind. She felt even more flustered than usual when picturing his face.

"Sorry, Jonas. Let's not talk about that right now."

Anne hurried into the house and saw Hugh sitting at a table waiting for them. Across from him were two chairs set up side by side.

The fairies and Salim, along with the doctor, were gathered around like an audience.

"All right, you two, take a seat. I want you to make your candy right in front of me."

There were bowls of water sitting on the table, one deep and one shallow for each of them. There were also two cutting boards that had been procured from the kitchen.

Looking at the items arranged before her, Anne frowned and sat down in one chair.

"You don't need to add any color. And I'll leave the decision of what to make up to you."

"Before we start, can I ask you something?"

Anne stared into Hugh's face from directly across the table.

"What is it?"

"Who are you? The way you arranged these tools…You couldn't have done it unless you're familiar with the process of making sugar candy. You wouldn't happen to be a candy crafter, too? Are you entering the Royal Candy Fair?"

Hugh's mouth curled into a suggestive smile. "If you want me to pay your lodging fees, hush and make candy, Anne."

"…Well, whatever. As long as you're paying."

Anne poured some of the water that had been set out on the table into the stone bowl that held her sugar.

Jonas started in the same way.

They added cold water to their silver sugar and kneaded the resulting mixture. As they did, the sugar became like a soft clay.

Normally, Anne would add colored powders into the dough to produce a variety of shades. It was the usual method crafters took, as combining various powders could make gorgeous, multicolored works of candy art. But this time, she wouldn't use any.

Anne transferred the claylike sugar dough to the cutting board and continued kneading.

Hugh hadn't laid out any of the tools for forming the candy, so there was nothing to do but make it using only her fingers.

Silver sugar melts easily from heat. Crafters must work quickly, cooling their hands with water while handling it.

Anne chilled her fingers in the cold water that had been set out on the table.

It is said that the hand movements of candy crafters are akin to those of magicians. They move gently and smoothly.

What should I make?

Anne thought it over as she kneaded her sugar.

I wonder what Mama would make if she was here?

Anne figured that Emma would probably have made good use of the white color and created something white.

Emma had loved plants, so Anne settled on a white flower.

Once she made her choice, she recalled a flower shape that Emma often crafted.

Anne molded the flower petals with her fingertips, producing a great number. Then, she layered them to make the flower.

Jonas was molding a cat that could sit in the palm of his hand. It had a long, elegant tail and a lovely curving body. It was obvious he was trying to show off.

Hugh stared at their hands as they worked, a serious expression on his face.

Cathy looked at Jonas's creation and marveled, "The things Master Jonas makes are truly incredible..."

It didn't take all that long for them to complete their tasks.

Anne and Jonas stopped working and lifted their heads at the same time.

"You two finished?" Hugh asked.

Jonas nodded confidently and pointed to his cutting board.

"All done."

"Me too."

Anne also placed the results of her efforts on her cutting board.

Hugh pulled the two boards toward him.

He looked back and forth between them for a while, then chuckled quietly.

"You're both pretty skilled. You don't seem like novice crafters at all."

Anne and Jonas looked at each other and smiled.

However, the very next moment, Hugh brought both his palms down and smashed their creations to bits.

"Ah!"

"What are you doing?!"

Anne and Jonas shouted.

Hugh stared at them with an unsparing expression.

"They were ugly, so I smashed them. Jonas, you've got nimble hands, but that's all you have. It was well-made, but since you just wanted to show off your skills, that's as far as you got. There was no creativity there. Anne, you did better than Jonas. But what was that? It was like you made an exact copy of something someone else already made. It was hollow; it had no spirit. I doubt eating something like that would draw in any good fortune or extend any fairy's life span. If this is all you can do, becoming a Silver Sugar Master is an impossible dream for either of you."

The lecture left both Anne and Jonas speechless.

Anne had a feeling that Hugh had hit the bull's-eye in some respects. He had accurately vocalized the feelings of inferiority that gnawed at her when she thought about her own work, feelings that had always been there but she'd never been able to articulate.

Jonas must have been in the same boat. His expression was stiff.

"Well, I guess I'll take these candy pieces with me. I can have them for a snack tomorrow."

Hugh swept the broken pieces of candy into a bowl and stood up.

"All right, then, off to bed, I suppose. I've got an early morning tomorrow. Come, Salim. See you later, Anne, Jonas. That was amusing—a good way to kill some time."

Hugh left the room with Salim.

The doctor was dumbfounded.

Cathy rushed over to the motionless Jonas. In her shrill voice, she cried, "What was that man trying to do?!" She hopped up on the table and stroked Jonas's hand. "Master Jonas, don't pay him any mind. You mustn't take the words of such a strange, suspicious man seriously!"

"Is that so?" Jonas smiled bitterly and glanced over at Anne. "I'm sorry, Anne. I...I'm going to my room."

"Me too... Good night!" Anne shouted.

She then took off running toward her own room.

She felt frustrated and intensely embarrassed.

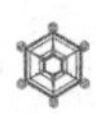

"Hey, you! Challe Fenn Challe! Are you thinking of going back to the room?!"

After watching Anne run away, Challe let out a sigh. He then started walking slowly in the same direction. He was turning in as well. Mithril called out to his back in a horrified tone.

Challe turned around and answered, "I am."

"Well, stop it!"

"What's wrong with going to the room?"

"After what that guy said, Anne must be really hurt. She might be crying, you know? Or if we're really unlucky, maybe she's flown into a rage?! She'll hate you if you just barge in like nothing happened!"

"I don't really care."

"We-well, I'm against it! I'm sleeping in the dining room tonight!"

"Do whatever you want."

As he walked back to the room, Challe mused that Hugh's appraisal had been spot-on.

Challe had felt the same way when he saw what Anne had made.

He thought that Anne herself probably agreed. That was why she was so hurt.

When he opened the door, the interior of the room was pitch-dark.

Anne had crawled into bed, covered herself from head to toe with her blanket, and curled up into a ball.

Challe sat down on the adjacent bed and gazed at the bundle of blankets.

Anne looked just like a bagworm.

Liz.

While staring at her, Challe suddenly remembered something.

When Liz was little…she also pouted and cried, and she often covered herself in her blanket and curled into a little ball. How old was she back then…? Maybe nine or ten? She stopped doing it after that.

He looked at the bagworm in front of him again.

This girl is fifteen?!

Even though Anne was fifteen years old, she could be terribly childish. The fact that she still acted that way was probably because, for years, she'd had a mother to protect her and give her a happy life.

When he pictured it, Challe felt like he was seeing the last embers of a dying fire. He found it kind of charming that Anne, who was always clamoring on about how grown-up she was, was acting like a child of ten. He chuckled to himself.

The moment he did, Anne sat up.

"What are you laughing at?! Is it that funny to see a person down in the dumps?!"

Her eyes were bright red and filled to the brim with tears. They glistened in the moonlight streaming through the window. She looked like she was trying hard not to let the tears overflow.

Holding back tears and biting her lip, she appeared all the more childish.

Challe knew it was wrong, but he snorted with laughter. He clapped one hand over his mouth.

"What?! Now you're laughing in my face?! In any case, a scarecrow like me isn't fit to be seen! I'm in here sobbing with grief, and you think my face looks funny. I've been mocked by people with beautiful faces like yours my whole life!" Anne shouted, then shoved her face back into her pillow.

Challe felt sorry for Anne. She seemed to be experiencing a lot of pain and turmoil. He himself felt very calm for some reason, though.

It was as if he had remembered something long buried.

Challe stood up and took a seat on the bed where Anne was lying.

That's right, Liz had hair this color when I first met her, too. I had forgotten.

Without really thinking, Challe picked up a tuft of Anne's hair that was spread out on the sheets.

"People won't mock you forever. Humans are different from us. Humans are always changing. I bet that before three years have passed, you'll turn out to be quite beautiful. Your hair will change color, too, into a light, beautiful golden blond. By then, no one will be calling you a scarecrow anymore. Your candy-crafting abilities will also develop. What Hugh said was not wrong, but you shouldn't worry about it."

Anne slowly, suspiciously lifted her face halfway off the pillow.

"I'm going to hone my skills at candy-making. I'm determined to get better. If I can get to where I'm going through hard work, I'll find a way. But I don't need you to comfort me with obvious lies about me becoming beautiful or whatever."

"It's not a lie. I know."

Challe looked down at the tuft of hair resting on his palm.

"When I was born, the first creature who laid eyes on me was a human child. A five-year-old girl. Her hair was the same color as yours. It seems I was born because of that girl's gaze."

It was a memory from long ago. For some reason, Challe wanted to share it. Some part of him harbored a faint hope that by doing so, he might regain something he had lost.

Anne looked surprised when Challe started telling the story.

"The girl was named Elizabeth...Liz for short. She was the daughter of a noble family, and due to her special circumstances, she was brought up separate from the outside world. She was young and ignorant. Liz knew nothing about fairies, so she mistakenly imagined that I was her older brother. She took me back home with her and gave me shelter."

Anne lifted her head from the pillow and sat up straight on the bed.

The lock of her hair slipped from Challe's grasp.

He slowly closed his now-empty hand, staring at his fist.

"From that point on, we were always together. After fifteen years, Liz's hair turned golden blond, her freckles faded, and she became a beautiful young woman. That's how I know. You will also change like Liz did."

"And then?"

Challe raised his head at Anne's question.

"What happened to Liz? You said Liz was always with you. Why isn't she here now?"

He cast his eyes back down.

The question made his chest hurt again, even though it had happened more than a hundred years earlier.

"She died... She was killed. The person who killed her was a human."

Anne hung her head when she heard his words.

After a moment, Anne's hand gently touched Challe's clenched fist.

"I'm sorry..."

He didn't understand why Anne was apologizing.

Perhaps she felt bad for making him share a sad memory.

Or perhaps it was an apology for the fact that she was a human, just like the one who had killed Liz.

But he could tell she had a kind heart.

Challe shook his head slightly and stood up. Anne's hand slipped off his fist.

He had said too much.

"Go to sleep already, scarecrow," Challe said quietly over his shoulder.

Memories are memories. No need to raise them.

When Anne awoke the following morning, Hugh had already departed. He had apparently left before dawn, but he had paid their lodging fees as promised.

Where on Earth did Hugh come from, I wonder?

But Anne didn't dwell too deeply on the question.

The impact of what Hugh had said to her had already mostly dissipated.

More importantly, the fragment of Challe's past that he had shared with her made a deep impression on Anne's heart.

The party set out from the Doctor's Inn. For three days, they traveled without any attacks from beasts or bandits.

During that time, Anne kept stealing glances at Challe's face as he sat next to her.

The warrior fairy had insisted he could never become friends with a human.

But when Challe was born, he bonded with a human girl.

They had spent fifteen years together, he'd said. That was a long time—the same amount of time Anne had spent with her mother.

To Challe, that girl Liz had probably been like family. But she was snatched away from him by human hands. It made Anne's heart ache to see the lonesome expression on Challe's face, his eyes downcast.

Challe had bonded with a human originally, and then humans had frozen his heart.

I wish there was some magic spell to thaw it again.

That was all Anne thought about as her wagon trundled along, her eyes constantly drawn to Challe's profile.

At the end of the seventh day after starting down the Bloody Highway, they arrived at a way station just as the evening sun was sinking in the sky.

They had made it two-thirds of the way down the road.

Anne closed the iron doors and breathed a sigh of relief.

If they traveled for three more days, they would be off the Bloody Highway.

Once they were safely inside the way station, Anne set about preparing dinner.

She ate a humble soup and an apple.

Jonas's dinner was fancy, as always.

Along the way, Jonas began trying to share his food with Anne, but she had refused every offer. It was dangerous to get accustomed to luxury on a journey. Since one never knew what might happen while traveling, it was important to ration food carefully and to get used to eating very basic meals.

Jonas retired to his wagon with Cathy in tow.

Mithril had finally stopped clamoring on about repaying his debt to Anne. He now perched atop the driver's seat all day as if he belonged there. At night, he gathered grass and made himself a little bed on top of the roof of the cargo hold, then slept there. That night as well, he diligently made his bed and was soon snoring away.

Anne still hadn't struck upon a method of repayment that would satisfy Mithril. He was probably going to stick with her forever until she did. She was already used to Mithril's shrill voice, and now that she was accustomed to it, his arrogance also seemed cute. It was odd.

Anne sat down near the fire with Challe and got ready to go to sleep.

Challe had set his apple on the palm of his hand and was eating it. The surface of the apple gradually wrinkled. It withered, then finally crumpled up into nothing and dissolved.

That was how fairies ate. No matter how many times Anne watched it, she still found it strange.

"It's kind of chilly tonight, huh? We should expect it to get cold as autumn draws to a close. Aren't you cold, Challe?"

"We don't feel the cold like humans do."

"Oh? That's handy."

The moment after she responded, Anne sneezed. It really was chilly.

Challe glanced over at the wagon where Jonas was sleeping and asked, "Why don't you sleep inside your cargo hold? You ought to sleep somewhere warm, like that boy does."

Anne pulled a blanket out from under the driver's seat and shook her head as she carried it over to the fireside.

"I don't know what Jonas uses his wagon for, but mine is a work area for making sugar candy. It's a sacred space. I can't sleep in a place like that. Mama and I never once slept inside the wagon. In winter, we went out of our way to find lodging elsewhere. Mama would always say, 'Sugar candy is a sacred food. We mustn't sully the places where it is made or the people who make it.'"

Staring into the fire, Challe responded, "She sounds like a good crafter, your mother."

When he said that, Anne recalled Emma's face. She felt extraordinarily lonely.

"Mm. Very good."

Anne didn't get much sleep that night.

I'm lonely.

Such feelings slowly rose to the surface of her heart again and again, like bubbles.

I wonder if Challe feels this way, too?

She tossed and turned, then looked over toward where Challe was lying.

He was just five or six steps away. She wished it was less.

Is he asleep? Or has he just got his eyes closed, thinking about something? I want to talk to him.

Anne extended her hand, driven by the impulse to touch his wing, which was spread out on the bed of grass.

She almost got up and reached for it but hesitated and stopped herself.

There's no telling what he'll say if I touch his wing while he's sleeping.

Challe was likely to be furious if a human touched his precious remaining wing.

A spell to melt Challe's heart…

Just then, she suddenly remembered the sugar candy.

She had promised to make him some, then completely forgotten about it when Mithril made his appearance.

Since she seemed unlikely to sleep anyway, Anne got up.

I'll make the candy I promised him.

Maybe the sweet sugar candy would warm Challe's heart just a little.

Anne opened the back doors to her cargo hold and stepped inside.

The light of the slightly-less-than-full moon streamed through the windows. Relying on it to see, Anne slid her hand softly over the cold stone worktable, touched the scales, and stroked the neatly arranged row of wooden spatulas.

Emma had been there. All the things that Emma had touched with her hands were waiting there quietly.

Thoughts of her mother came to her in the silence, threatening to make Anne lose her composure.

She shook her head and surveyed the barrels of silver sugar.

"We made candy for Hugh, but there should be plenty of silver sugar left. I bet I can make two or three pieces to give to Challe," she mumbled as she opened the lid on one of the barrels.

"Huh?"

As far as Anne remembered, the barrel she opened had been more than half full of silver sugar.

But it was empty. She wondered whether she had mistakenly opened the wrong one.

With that thought, she opened the lid on the barrel she had thought was empty. There was nothing in that one, either.

"But…how?"

Anne was dumbfounded. Her heart beat faster.

One after another, she opened the remaining barrels. The three others were packed to the brim with sugar, just as she had left them.

But two out of the five were completely depleted.

The ingredient she needed to make her entry for the Royal Candy Fair was gone.

Chapter 5
THE SUGAR APPLE IS A DECEITFUL TREE

Anne sank to her knees, clutching the rim of one of the empty barrels.

"No way. Why isn't it here? When we used the sugar at the Doctor's Inn, this barrel was more than half full… I checked it. And then I locked the doors to the cargo hold."

Even if they made it to Lewiston on time, Anne wouldn't be able to enter the Royal Candy Fair.

If she used any of the remaining sugar, her three barrels would be underweight, and she would be disqualified. But having three full barrels of silver sugar wouldn't mean much if she didn't have anything to make candy with.

"…Why…why?! No one has been in here! How?!" Anne shouted.

"What are you fussing about?"

Challe's voice came from outside the open door.

Anne stood up. Her legs were weak and unsteady. She felt like she was treading on a path piled high with fallen leaves. She staggered as soon as she stepped out of the wagon, then she crouched down in front of Challe.

"What happened?"

"My silver sugar… It's gone."

"Gone?"

"…I've got three barrels left. But in order to enter the candy fair, I need those three barrels, plus my candy. And the silver sugar I was supposed to use to make it is gone…"

Challe frowned.

"You had it at the Doctor's Inn?"

"I had it then. I checked. And I know I locked the doors. No one should have been able to go in or out, and yet..."

Yet the silver sugar had disappeared.

Anne's hands trembled slightly as she gripped Challe's sleeve. Her vision was blurry.

She didn't understand how her stores had vanished.

"Anne? Did something happen?"

Jonas must have heard her voice, and he emerged from his wagon with Cathy. When he saw Anne crouched on the ground, he tilted his head quizzically.

Anne feared that her tears would spill over if she tried to speak, so she didn't answer. In her place, Challe said, "Apparently, the silver sugar is gone."

"Huh? But your silver sugar was in your cargo hold, right? And the doors were locked; no one could go in or out?"

"...No. It was possible to get in and out."

The one who broodingly said this was Cathy.

Everyone's eyes focused on her as the implication behind her words dawned on them.

"What does that mean, Cathy?"

She hung her head at Jonas's question.

"I don't want to say something that will betray a member of my own kind, but...I saw it. The night that we stayed at the Doctor's Inn, I saw it from the window of our room. There are windows up high in the cargo hold of Ms. Anne's wagon, right? I saw Mithril Lid Pod coming out of one of them. In the moonlight, his whole body looked like it was glittering. He was covered in silver sugar."

Mithril...?

"What's going on down there? You're being awfully loud. And everyone's here. What are you talking about?"

Rubbing his sleepy eyes, Mithril peered down at them from the roof of the cargo hold.

It couldn't be. But only someone small like a little fairy could get in and out of the locked cargo hold. Moreover, that night, Mithril was indeed the only one who slept in the dining room.

Anne stared up at Mithril's face. She wanted to believe he was incapable of having done such a thing.

"Mithril, come down here," Jonas ordered strictly.

"What the heck? I'm not under your control! Don't act all important. And don't abbreviate my name. I'm Mithril Lid Pod..."

"Get down here!!"

Mithril was immediately frightened by Jonas's sudden intensity. Once he had descended from the roof, he looked up nervously at Anne.

"Wh-what is it?"

"Do you like silver sugar?" Jonas asked.

Mithril nodded. "I do. Are there any fairies who dislike it? What kind of question is that? What of it anyway?"

"The night that we stayed at the Doctor's Inn, you and you alone slept in the dining room, is that right? Will you deny that you did so with an ulterior motive?"

"Huh?"

"Some of the silver sugar that Anne had prepared for the Royal Candy Fair has gone missing. The night that we stayed at the Doctor's Inn, Cathy saw you coming out of the cargo hold of Anne's wagon, covered in silver sugar."

Mithril blinked in surprise. His mouth opened and closed several times. Then, he immediately lost his cool and started shouting at Cathy.

"Wh-what is this?! What did you tell them? We're both fairies! And you told them that I did something like that?!"

Cathy hid behind Jonas and said in a feeble voice, "Because I saw you do it."

"Liar!" Mithril shouted, turning back toward Anne.

He regarded her with fear in his eyes.

"Anne. I was not the one who stole your silver sugar. Cathy is lying."

"What would Cathy stand to gain by lying?"

"Silence, human!!" Mithril yelled, cutting off Jonas's reproachful words.

He pleaded with Anne again.

"Anne, don't tell me you suspect me, too? It wasn't me. I swear it wasn't me!"

Mithril strung his words together nervously.

Anne wanted to believe him, but she also had no evidence that would dispel the accusation.

Maybe… No, it can't be. He wouldn't do that… But…

Suspicions swirled through Anne's mind. She wanted to believe Mithril, but on the other hand, maybe…

Anne's feelings must have shown on her face.

Tears welled up in Mithril's eyes as he looked at her.

"You suspect me, don't you, Anne? You don't believe me…Anne."

"…I want to believe you."

"But you don't, do you?! You doubt me just a little bit."

Tears spilled from Mithril's eyes.

"Fine, if you're going to look at me with those doubting eyes, then… I'll just disappear from your sight!" Mithril shouted, then he leaped as hard as he could into the air and disappeared to the other side of the wagon.

"Mithril, wai—…"

Anne started calling out to stop him, but her voice broke off in the middle. She didn't have any business calling him back when she didn't really trust him. If she tried to tell him she believed him before she could wipe the distrustful look off her face, it would only hurt him more.

Anne's body gave out, and she lost all strength. She let go of Challe's sleeve and sat down with a *thump* on the stairs of the cargo hold. She covered her face with both hands.

"Now…I can't enter this year's candy fair…"

Challe was silent and looked off in the direction that Mithril had fled.

Jonas put his hand to his chin. Then after a few moments, he clapped his hands loudly.

"That's it! Listen, Anne, don't give up! You only have to make one piece of candy. Can't we refine just enough silver sugar to do that before we arrive?"

"No way. First of all, I don't even have sugar apples, the raw ingredient."

"Oh, we've got sugar apples! I heard about this once at a Radcliffe Workshop meeting. There's a sugar-apple grove that grows alongside the Bloody Highway. Though apparently, no one ever goes there to pick apples, since they would have to spend all their profits paying for protection just to get there. It's autumn now, so the trees should have fruit!"

Sugar-apple trees are mysterious things.

Trees cultivated by human hands never bear fruit.

Only those growing wild produce fruit.

Because of that, candy crafters are obsessed with knowing where sugar-apple tree groves are located and how to obtain their fruit.

If this grove had been a topic of discussion at a meeting of the Radcliffe Workshop, it was most likely true.

However—

"Even if we get sugar apples, it will take me three days to refine them. I won't have time to make it to Lewiston and produce my piece for the competition."

"Well, how about during the three days it takes to refine the silver sugar, you use the sugar you have left to create your candy? You can do both at the same time. Then once your entry is finished and you've refined enough silver sugar to replace what you've used, all that will be left is to travel the rest of the way to Lewiston."

"I could never…"

She had been about to say she could never do such a thing, but finally, Anne's mind started working again.

It just might be possible.

She raised her head and looked at Jonas. He nodded encouragingly.

"You can do it. Cheer up, Anne. I'm an amateur candy crafter, too, so I can help you."

Jonas put a reassuring hand on her shoulder. She was overwhelmed with gratitude for his kindness and for the information she needed to get out of her current predicament.

"Thank you, Jonas."

Finally, Anne was able to smile just a little. She then looked up at Challe.

"I'm sorry, Challe. I kind of lost my head. And you were sleeping, too. Sorry for waking you."

"It's fine," Challe said before turning his back coldly on Anne and returning to the fireside.

Anne and Jonas spread out a map on top of the driver's seat of her wagon.

"If I'm not mistaken, there should be a sugar-apple grove in this area. It's close to a way station. From there, you can refine the sugar and make it to Lewiston in no time," Jonas said, pointing to a spot on the map.

The place he indicated was half a day away from Lewiston by horse-drawn wagon. Luckily, it was near a way station.

Ideally, Anne would have liked to harvest the sugar apples, then refine them into silver sugar after they were off the Bloody Highway. That would be safer.

However, if sugar apples are not refined immediately after harvesting, they'll retain their characteristic bitterness. Sugar apples that spent even half a day jostling around in Anne's carriage would never become fine silver sugar.

That meant Anne would have no choice but to stay at the nearby way station and refine the necessary quantity of silver sugar there.

From their present location, it would take three days to reach the sugar-apple grove.

It would take another day to find and harvest the fruit.

From there, three days to refine the sugar at the way station.

And half a day to get from the station to Lewiston.

The Royal Candy Fair was eight days away, and that included the day of the fair itself.

It would be close.

But not impossible.

Anne stared at the map with fresh determination.

"We'll do our best, Anne."

With that last word of encouragement, Jonas withdrew to his own wagon, accompanied by Cathy.

Anne returned to the fireside.

She had already settled down quite a lot.

She seated herself next to Challe and explained simply what she had discussed with Jonas.

When she finished, Anne hugged her knees to her chest and rested her chin on top of them.

After silence had descended over the camp, Anne slowly looked around at her surroundings. Mithril was nowhere to be seen.

"Hey, where's Mithril?"

Tossing some twigs into the nearly extinguished fire, Challe answered, "Gone."

"Where...did he go...?"

Anne cast her eyes down, tore up some dead grass, and threw it in the fire.

With a *crackle*, the grass burned instantly.

Even if Mithril was the culprit who had stolen her silver sugar, Anne thought it would have demonstrated real trust if she had believed him when he insisted he didn't do it. She knew she'd come across like a prejudiced human when she doubted his word.

She felt even more miserable about it because she was just starting to find Mithril cute.

"Was it really him?" Challe muttered.

Anne raised her face. "Was who what?"

"Was it really Mithril who stole from you?" Challe mumbled doubtfully with a slight scowl.

Considering the circumstances, it would have been impossible for anyone but Mithril to have done it.

But Challe had a point. It was hard to imagine why Mithril, who had been so keen to repay his favor to Anne that he'd followed her all this way, would do something so thoughtless. Perhaps he had succumbed to the sweet temptation of the silver sugar.

Or perhaps it had been someone else.

But Anne also didn't want to think Cathy was lying.

"I don't know… I don't know who really stole the silver sugar… The more important thing now is obtaining the sugar apples. I'm going to enter this year's candy fair, no matter what… I'm sorry. I forgot to make the sugar candy I promised I would make you, Challe. Well, I remembered and was about to make it, but…now I'm going to have to postpone that for a little while. But when I give back your wing, I'll add some candy as a present along with it. I promise."

As she said that, Anne crawled into her cot and pulled the blanket up over herself. Challe just sat there quietly.

Will I make it in time? Please let me make it somehow. Please, Mama.

Challe Fenn Challe sat gazing into the fire.

It didn't make sense. How had the silver sugar disappeared?

Considering the circumstances, the most likely possibility was that Mithril had eaten it.

But Mithril didn't seem like the culprit to Challe.

He was noisy and annoying, but Mithril was grateful to Anne from the bottom of his heart. Challe did not believe he would have done something so thoughtless, knowing how much trouble it would cause for Anne.

But if it wasn't Mithril...then who?

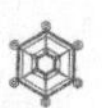

For three days, Anne drove her boxy wagon onward, thinking only of making progress.

She hardly even took breaks for lunch.

It was dangerous to travel at night, so they couldn't move the wagons after dark. They took refuge at the way stations and impatiently waited for dawn.

Fortunately, the party suffered no attacks from bandits or beasts, and a little past noon on the third day, they arrived at the way station that was supposed to be close to the sugar-apple grove.

Another half a day of riding would take them to the royal capital.

The final way station sat atop a small hill. From there, Anne could look out over the wilderness, far into the distance. Past the sparse forest and the big, meandering river, she could see the spires of the royal castle, small on the horizon.

It struck her that Lewiston was close at hand.

But close though her destination may have been, Anne could not leave just yet. She clenched her fists.

I've got to get my hands on those sugar apples quickly.

The following day, Anne set out in one of the carriages with Jonas at first light.

They left the highway and rode about checking the many stands of trees that were scattered around the forest, searching for the sugar-apple grove.

Then when the sun was high in the sky, bright-red fruit caught Anne's eye.

"…Sugar apples."

Anne felt so relieved that her legs threatened to give out under her.

The sugar-apple trees were short. The tallest of them only reached as high as the top of Anne's head.

The trees were dainty, with countless branches about the size of human fingers stretching out from their slender trunks. On the tips of those slim branches were deep-crimson fruits, each about the size of a chicken egg. They looked a lot like ordinary apples. They were glossy and red, like they had been varnished with wax.

Anne felt a surge of motivation after their surprisingly quick discovery of the sugar apples.

"I'm going to make it. If I work on my entry while I refine these sugar apples, I can make it to Lewiston with time to spare!"

She leaped down off the driver's seat and pulled out a basket from her wagon.

Anne tossed one apple after another into her basket, and Jonas helped, too.

When it was full, they quickly transferred the apples to the cargo hold and refilled the basket. After repeating that five or six times, the floor of the cargo hold was so buried in shades of red that there was no place left to step.

Anne cheered up at the sight of the red color of the sugar apples. Emma had often said she felt the same way.

For three days, they had dashed down the Bloody Highway to find this grove.

In her haste, Anne had let the gloomy feelings about Mithril and how she'd treated him fall by the wayside.

She was looking forward, not back. As long as she had hope, she would charge ahead without hesitation.

If she worked hard, she could make it in time.

"Let's get to work!"

Anne rolled up her sleeves as soon as they got back to the way station with a wagon full of sugar apples.

As she retrieved a huge pot and ladle out of the cargo hold, Anne spoke to Challe, who was lying down on the driver's seat, dangling his long legs over the side.

"Once I make my entry piece for the candy fair, I'm going to make some candy to give to you right away, Challe. Just wait, okay?"

"Something edible, please."

Anne laughed off his rude response.

"I told you, I'll show you my skills!" Anne answered in a lively voice. She started tossing the sugar apples into the big pot, humming as she went.

Challe sat up a little bit and watched Anne happily working away.

The sugar apple tree is said to be deceitful.

It grows bright-red, glossy, delicious-looking fruits. They can be turned into precious silver sugar. However, if one bites into a piece of that same fruit, it is extremely bitter and astringent, completely inedible. The tree grows fruit that betrays all expectations.

In the hands of candy crafters, even that treacherous fruit is transformed into the purest sweetness.

To make silver sugar, one must first fill a large pot with water and add a handful of silver sugar, then place the freshly harvested sugar apples into the pot and leave them to soak for a whole day and night. Doing so removes the bitterness.

Toss out that water, refill the pot with fresh water, and place it over a fire.

The sugar apples fall apart during cooking, so when the seeds and skin come floating to the surface, scoop them out along with any scum and boil down the rest.

When the mixture becomes syrupy, transfer it from the pot to a level stone slab. Spread it evenly, then let it dry for another full day and night.

When it dries, it will change color and form pure-white lumps. The final step is to grind the lumps in a mortar and make a powder.

Then the silver sugar is done. It will be bright white with a slight tinge of blue.

Compared with sugar refined from sugarcane, which has a yellow tinge and a strong taste, the fine grain and powdery texture of silver sugar has a pale color and a fresh sweetness to it, leaving a nice aftertaste. It is truly a sacred food.

Once she was done putting her crop of sugar apples in water to soak,

Anne immediately set to work making the candy she would present at the Royal Candy Fair.

One of the requirements was to make a large piece that could be used as part of the festival.

She went into her cargo hold and pulled a sheaf of papers out from under the workbench. The papers, all different sizes and shapes and yellowed with age, were bound together with a string. Anne untied the string and spread the papers out on top of the workbench.

The pages contained notes and designs for sugar-candy sculptures. The sketches had been drawn with a crude quill pen, so the lines were blurry and jagged. The color schemes and explanations of the shapes were written in messy handwriting.

Emma had compiled this collection of designs over many years. Whenever she made a piece of sugar candy, she would first lay out these schematics before choosing one from among them.

"These are your mama's prized possessions. I made them myself. We can never share them with anyone. I mustn't let anybody copy me," Emma had said about the bundle of papers.

While they were on the road, they'd sold the candies Anne made at a reasonable price to customers who wanted cheap sugar candy. She had made her candies according to these designs at Emma's direction.

Now Emma wasn't around to tell her which to use.

Anne would have to choose for herself.

After pondering for a while, Anne selected one with a flower motif that Emma had particularly loved. The flower was light pink, and its leaves were light green. White and blue butterflies were perched on the blossom. It was a lovely design.

Just when she'd made her selection, Anne suddenly recalled the words of Hugh, whom they'd met at the Doctor's Inn.

He'd called her work an imitation.

Well then, what should I make, and how, to avoid another imitation? I don't know…

As she thought it over, Anne set the yellowed papers down on top of the workbench and pulled out vials of powder colored red, green, and blue.

She chilled her hands with water from a bucket, then picked up a stone bowl and walked over to the barrels full of silver sugar.

She was about to scoop some from one of the barrels, when—
"Anne? Anne?"
—someone knocked on the door to the cargo hold and then opened it. Jonas poked his head in.
"Do you have enough barrels to hold the refined silver sugar? I had an extra in my wagon; do you want to use it?"
Holding one small barrel, Jonas stepped up into Anne's cargo hold.
Anne smiled wryly.
"The apples are still soaking. It'll be a while before they're refined. Besides, I've got two empty barrels."
"Ah, right. Well, I already brought this one over, so I'll leave it right here."
When Jonas set the barrel down underneath the workbench, the floor shook. Anne was startled by the quake.
"Are you sure that's empty? It seems super heavy. Is it made of really thick wood?"
"I brought it from my father's workshop, so it's first-rate craftsmanship. It'll protect your silver sugar from getting damp."
"Thank you. But why did you bring something like that on a trip?"
"I just had a feeling we might need it. More importantly, have you decided what you're going to make?'
"Mm-hmm. I'm going to try to finish it before the sugar apples floating in the water are refined into silver sugar."
"I'm expecting something great."
Jonas softly approached Anne and put his hand on her cheek.
"Wh-what?!" Anne jumped back in surprise.
With a bitter smile, Jonas approached again.
"Do your best, Anne."
Jonas placed both hands on Anne's shoulders and brought his face close to the tip of her nose, so close that she could feel his breath.
Without thinking, Anne held the stone bowl in her hand up to cover her face.
"Wh-wh-what?! Jonas?! Hold on, what is this? Stop it!"
"Don't be so unromantic, Anne."
With one hand, Jonas pushed the stone bowl back down, and with the other, he embraced her waist. Jonas smiled.

"I love you, Anne."

"I don't feel the same way!"

"I love you."

He brought his lips toward hers.

"N-no!"

Anne struck Jonas's cheek with an open hand.

Jonas put his hand to his cheek in surprise, released Anne, and stepped back.

"Why, Anne?"

"I am not in love with you, Jonas!"

"But I love you!"

"Those are your feelings!! They've got nothing to do with me!" Anne shouted.

She realized that she didn't have even the slightest stir of love toward Jonas.

Her heart had fluttered, and she had gotten flustered by his proposals and kind words. But the moment he actually pulled her in for a kiss, what she felt was fear.

Jonas looked like he didn't believe it. That was probably only natural.

He had been the most popular boy in the village since he was young. All the girls got worked up wanting to be his girlfriend. Jonas probably thought that all girls liked him.

"I see. I was hoping you had fallen for me."

Jonas smiled slightly, looking hurt. At that point, Anne regained her composure.

"...Ah...sorry. I...kind of...hit you."

"It's fine. I was being pushy... Oh yeah! It'd be a waste of time for you to fix meals while you've got work to do, right? I'll bring you something to eat in a bit."

"Sure. Thanks."

Jonas smiled again and left. Anne let out a big sigh.

Worrying about her meals even after she'd slapped him showed what a good person Jonas was, she thought.

"If I had fallen in love with Jonas, I doubt I would have ever gone through with anything like this," Anne muttered, returning to her work.

As she was scooping the silver sugar from the barrel, she heard another knock, and the door opened again.

This time, it was Cathy, dragging a big basket along with her.

"This is from Master Jonas. He told me to deliver some food to you. Where should I leave it?"

"Thank you, Cathy. Put it under the workbench over there. I'll eat it later."

Anne kept measuring the silver sugar without looking up. Cathy lightly jumped onto the workbench.

"Let me give you a bit of advice."

When Anne looked up, she saw Cathy was making a very hostile expression.

"I know you're feeling pretty full of yourself now that Master Jonas has proposed to you and told you he loves you."

"Huh? …I don't remember feeling that way…"

Anne was bewildered by Cathy's sudden accusation.

"You don't seriously think that Master Jonas is really in love with a girl like you, do you?"

Anne cocked her head on hearing those hurtful words. She had the feeling she had seen a similar expression and heard similar words before.

Where was that…? I think back in Knoxberry Village…

She suddenly remembered.

"Cathy, are you by any chance…in love with Jonas?"

Cathy's cheeks instantly blushed redder than her own red hair.

"What did you say?!"

Her voice cracked, too. Cathy acted just like the girls of Knoxberry. The same girls who had been jealous of Anne for renting a room in Jonas's house. They had often made irrational and nasty remarks toward her.

The realization made Anne smile.

"How nice. You must be happy that the person you love has your other wing. That's so much better than if it was being held by some jerk who makes fun of you or someone you hate, right?"

"We're not talking about this! I was telling you not to get conceited…"

"I think it would be wonderful if love between a fairy and a human could be realized."

"You are really an idiot! I can't talk to you!"

Cathy squared her shoulders and left the wagon in a huff.

Compared with Cathy, I feel really sorry for Challe. I'm in possession of his wing, and he's convinced I'm a fool.

Through the gap in the wagon doors, Anne could see Challe's back as he sat by the campfire.

His wing, draped smoothly over the grass, reflected the brightness of the flames and shone like brilliant rubies.

"Love between a fairy and a human..."

Suddenly, a thought came to her. The human girl, Liz, whom Challe had once bonded with—might they have been in love with each other? The moment the thought occurred to Anne, she felt a sharp pang in her chest.

She didn't really understand where the pain was coming from. It made her suspicious of her own feelings.

"...What's going on...?"

For some reason, Anne felt intensely jealous of Liz, the girl in Challe's memories.

At any rate, I am Challe's master in the end. The only reason he's with me is because I have his wing. That's why I have to keep my promise and release him once we arrive in Lewiston.

When she thought that, Anne felt as if a cold wind had blown across her chest. The wind whispered to her faintly: *You'll miss him...*

Anne acted as if she didn't hear it, shook it off, and got back to work.

Anne added cold water to the silver sugar and kneaded it. The sugar became like soft clay.

She mixed powders into the dough to color it. She repeated this many times over, dyeing each section.

She shaped the dough, shaving it down with a spatula. She flattened some out with a rolling pin and rolled other bits into balls.

Using various techniques, Anne proceeded to create sugar candy out of the powdery silver sugar.

She changed the water for the sugar apples and started the work of boiling them down.

Anne left the door to her wagon standing open and jumped down out of the cargo hold periodically to stir the pot and remove scum and apple peels. Then, she would head back to the wagon and keep working on her candy.

Jonas occasionally peeked into Anne's wagon, but he never said anything. Once he saw that she was still working, he left silently.

Anne felt awkward, too, so she wasn't particularly inclined to talk to him, either.

From time to time, she could hear the howling of wolves.

But being inside the way station gave her a sense of security, so she didn't pay them much mind.

Once the sugar apples boiled down, she transferred the pulp to a flat stone vessel and spread it out evenly.

On the second day, Anne continued working, hardly stopping to rest. She ate her meals while she stirred the pot and only lay down for two or three hours of sleep.

Because of her efforts, her candy quickly took shape.

It looked exactly like something Emma would have made. Anne had re-created her mother's delicate workmanship from memory.

The color of the multihued flower petals changed in a soft gradient. The fretwork on the butterflies' wings formed geometric patterns. The molding on the leaves created gentle curves. It was such a large piece of sugar candy that Anne could barely wrap her arms around it. With such an enormous piece, it was difficult to achieve an overall balance. But Anne had managed that brilliantly as well.

On the morning of the third day after she began, Anne's work of candy art was complete.

The result was good, and Anne was proud. The piece itself was perfect.

But Anne couldn't shake a vague sense of discomfort.

It was supposed to be exactly the same as a piece that Emma had made. Yet Anne had a feeling her work lacked the magnetism Emma's always had that captured peoples' attention.

Blind imitation.

Those words flashed through her mind again and again.

But her technique was perfect. Anne told herself it was fine.

She tied strings around the base of the sugar-candy sculpture, then anchored it in place on her workbench. That way, even as the wagon swayed, it wouldn't fall and break.

When that was done, Anne breathed a sigh of relief.

After working hard for days, she staggered down from her wagon.

"I'm exhausted."

She flopped down beside Challe, who was lying in the grass, staring up at the sky.

"Are you finished?" Challe managed to ask without sounding the least bit interested.

Anne nodded and stretched out on the grass.

Studying the withered color of the autumn blades, Anne counted the days.

"Including today, we have two more days until the Royal Candy Fair. This afternoon, I'll mill the partially refined silver sugar that's drying now and finish it up. Then if we head out tomorrow, we can get to Lewiston the day before the candy fair. I'll have my entry and my three barrels of silver sugar all together. Thank goodness."

The thought made Anne break into a smile.

The wind blew, making the grass rustle.

"I was curious," Challe said quietly.

"About what?"

"When I first met you in the fairy market, you had the sweet scent of silver sugar. I thought it was strange and wondered why that was."

"Oh? Maybe it had soaked into my dress."

Anne sniffed several times and smelled the cuffs of her sleeves. Challe shook his head.

"It's your fingers. Your fingers have a sweet scent."

"My fingers don't smell!"

"I can smell it."

"Really…? Well, I am always handling silver sugar. I suppose that must be why."

Feeling peaceful, Anne lay there absentmindedly for a while. Challe's wing was spread out over the low grass in front of her. It reflected the light of the sun and shone a pale-green color. She was staring at its brilliance when she heard the sound of footsteps on the grass, approaching from behind.

"Anne. Great job. I took a peek inside your cargo hold. That's really incredible. I've never seen such a large yet delicate sugar candy before. There's no question it'll earn a royal medal."

Jonas's kind words flowed out.

Anne was completely exhausted, so without lifting her head, she simply thanked him.

"Thank you. It was only possible because you knew about the sugar apples."

"No, thank you."

Jonas smirked and walked off toward Anne's wagon.

What is he thanking me for? Anne wondered as she sat up.

She saw that Jonas was hitching his horse to her wagon.

"What are you doing, Jonas?"

"I thought I'd head out now."

Challe frowned and sat up as well.

"You're too early, Jonas. The silver sugar isn't finished yet. We'll leave tomorrow. Besides, that's not even my horse," Anne said.

"It's fine. My horse can run faster. Good-bye."

"Jonas?"

Expressionless, Jonas finished hooking up his horse and climbed into the driver's seat of Anne's carriage.

Anne thought he was acting strangely, and she got to her feet. She began walking toward him.

"Jonas? What is this?"

"If only you had fallen for me and agreed to be my bride, I wouldn't have had to resort to something like this. But it's all your fault. I confessed my love to you three times, you know. And you rejected me."

That moment—

—the iron doors of the way station's gate swung open with great force.

Cathy came flying in, looking frantic. She was holding a lump of bloody meat. She came bounding toward Anne at full speed, making leap after enormous leap.

Anne could hear the footfalls of many wild beasts pursuing her.

Challe leaped up, his eyes wide.

"What's the meaning of this?!"

As he shouted, he stretched out his right hand, summoning his sword.

The same moment that Challe's blade materialized, the beasts, baying and growling, burst into the way station. It was a pack of wolves. Thirty of them.

Anne was petrified.

In front of her face, Cathy shrieked, "I told you not to be so full of yourself!"

She then threw the chunk of bloody meat, aiming directly at Anne's chest.

The moment she released it, Cathy took an even larger leap. She landed on the cargo hold of Anne's carriage.

Following the scent, the wolves all rushed Anne at once.

She didn't even have a chance to scream.

Challe jumped between her and the pack.

With one swing of his sword, he killed three wolves.

The rest quickly spread out, surrounding Anne and growling.

"Challe. What…? This…?"

"They lured them here, those two."

Those two? Jonas and Cathy? Why would they…?

Jonas whipped the horse. At the sound, Anne snapped out of her daze and realized what was happening.

Jonas is trying to steal my sugar candy!

Anne forgot she was surrounded by deadly predators, and without thinking, she broke into a run.

"Jonas!!"

The wagon had already started rolling. Anne chased after it, trying to jump up on the driver's seat.

At the reins, Jonas pulled a large vial from his breast pocket. He sent the cork plug flying with his thumb and dumped the contents onto Anne's head.

She was doused with a thick, foul-smelling, dark-red liquid.

Anne paid it no mind and desperately grabbed the hem of Jonas's jacket.

The wolves reacted to the liquid covering Anne. They'd surrounded Challe but quickly moved to pounce on her again.

Challe clicked his tongue and slashed through the wolves bearing down on his master, but, frenzied, they charged her again and again with wild eyes.

"Wait!!"

"Bye-bye, Anne."

The whip came down, aiming for the hand still clutching Jonas's jacket hem. An intense pain bit into her, and she let go.

Without her hold, the momentum threw her down on the grass, as if the wagon itself had shaken her off as it sped away. The wolves leaped forward, aiming for the fallen Anne. Challe jumped in their path.

Anne shouted at his back as he whittled down the pack.

"Challe! Chase after Jonas! Go! Quickly!"

"If I leave, you'll be wolf food!"

"It's fine. I don't care! Go! Get it back! My candy!!"

"I refuse."

Bathed in blood, Challe didn't stop moving even for a moment and continued slaughtering the wolves.

His wing flowed through the air, following his movements. The wolves tried to catch it. The beasts knew about the weaknesses of fairies.

Just before their fangs closed on his wing, Challe twisted his body and dodged, then swung his sword.

"Get it back, get it back!! Follow him!! Please, please, Challe, listen to what I'm saying!"

"Order me, then! Like a master would!!"

I'll tear your wing. I'll crush your wing. No matter how she tried, such cruel words wouldn't come out of Anne's mouth.

"Please go after him!"

All Anne could manage was to raise her voice.

"Challe! Chase him, chase him!! Please chase him!! Please!! Please!!"

The wagon carrying Anne's candy sculpture sped away.

Challe Fenn Challe stood stock-still, staring down at the corpses of the slain wolves littered at his feet.

He was out of breath after a hard fight. Blood spattered his lone wing. He gave it a quick shake, flicking off the viscera.

The wolves had persistently targeted his wing, and several times, he'd felt a surge of fear.

Anne was in a daze, sitting motionless in the sea of blood.

Challe was relieved that his wing and Anne were safe.

With a swing, he dissipated his sword and approached Anne.

"...Why didn't you go after him for me?"

Anne stared at the open door of the way station where the wagon had passed, wearing a blank expression on her face.

"If I had chased Jonas, you would have been killed and eaten by the wolves."

"I know that!"

Suddenly, Anne stood up and walked toward Challe.

"I know that! But you made that decision, not me! I didn't want him to steal my candy, even if it meant getting eaten by wolves. You don't listen to my orders at all. That's always been the case since we started this journey. Ultimately, you just do whatever you feel like. Isn't that right?! You refused to leave my side because I still have your wing, that's all. Earlier, if you'd chased after my candy sculpture, I might have been killed and eaten by the wolves. And if that had happened, your wing might have been damaged, too, right? So you protected me over my candy. That's all it was. I get it. I can't control you! That's why things ended up like this!" Anne shouted and pounded Challe's chest with both fists as hard as she could.

Over and over again, she struck him. She kept on hitting until she wore herself out and the strength had left her arms.

Anne's accusations were absurd. But she believed them. Despite how unreasonable she was being, Challe knew Anne probably wasn't going to back down until she got out what she needed to say. So he let her do as she pleased.

Finally, Anne's arms dropped. Her eyes still cast downward, she staggered over to the cargo hold of the wagon Jonas had left behind, and she crawled inside.

She's right. I haven't followed her orders, not once.

Challe had saved Anne from danger several times on their journey for no other reason than the fact that she possessed his wing. If she got hurt, so would it. As a result, he had no choice but to protect her.

However, earlier, the moment that the wolves had sprung at her—

—it hadn't even occurred to him that his wing might be damaged.

His body had moved instantly to shield Anne as she sat there in a daze.

A drop of something cold fell onto his cheek.

He looked up and saw it was a drop of rain, fallen from a darkening sky. Like someone's tears.

Chapter 6
BORN IN THE MORNING

In the darkness, a cold drizzling rain fell.

Challe had moved the wolf carcasses outside the way station.

Still, the damp smell of rain and blood lingered.

The wolves had trampled the partially refined silver sugar, and it became filthy with their blood even before mixing with rainwater. Raindrops sent ripples through the slush.

Anne sat inside the wagon Jonas had left behind.

The interior of the cargo hold was set up exactly like Anne's. It was a workshop for making sugar candy.

The broken remains of half-completed candies lay scattered on the floor.

The top of the workbench was littered with papers covered in candy designs. All of them looked to be copies of the candy designs Emma had left behind.

Inside the cargo hold were also five barrels, and all were packed with silver sugar.

It was premeditated from the very beginning. Everything he said was a lie…

Jonas was in a position to become the next maestro of the Radcliffe Workshop. But in order for that to happen, he had to become a Silver Sugar Master first.

He had told her that he'd entered the Royal Candy Fair twice in the past but had yet to become a Silver Sugar Master. That despite his prior losses, he wasn't planning to participate in the candy fair this year.

She ought to have been suspicious of that.

Jonas had probably lost his confidence because of his previous failures.

But he wanted to achieve the rank of Silver Sugar Master, even if that meant resorting to theft. Once he achieved that title, he would have the chance to become the maestro of the Radcliffe Workshop. He might even become the Silver Sugar Viscount, as he'd always hoped.

The sort of people who earn royal medals and become Silver Sugar Masters are those with a sincere love for sugar candy, for whom profits are a secondary consideration. Only people like that can create splendid works of candy art.

Jonas only seemed concerned with glory.

Even if he did become a Silver Sugar Master, he would never care all that much about candy. He didn't take it seriously.

Jonas must have been worrying about his future when a sick and helpless Silver Sugar Master and her daughter fell right into his lap.

He had obviously decided to put them to use.

First, he had stolen into Emma and Anne's wagon and plagiarized Emma's candy designs.

But even with those designs, he'd been incapable of making the candy to his satisfaction. Though confident in his talents, he had no confidence in the candies he created.

"That was why he proposed to me…"

The reason Jonas had proposed to Anne was to coax her into making sugar candy for him, to enable him to obtain the title of Silver Sugar Master on the back of her work.

But there, too, Jonas had failed.

That must have been when he'd had the idea of stealing Anne's candy and entering it as his own creation for the Royal Candy Fair.

The people of the Anders household had fully supported this plan.

Jonas's parents had provided their son with a wagon and bodyguards for his scheme.

If their son became the maestro of the Radcliffe Workshop, it would bring great prosperity to the whole Anders family.

Then, Jonas had followed Anne to the candy fair, journeyed with her, and stolen a portion of her silver sugar.

Cathy was probably the one who had actually stolen the sugar. She had the power to turn invisible. So the night that they stayed at the Doctor's Inn, she must have sneaked in through the high windows and carried the silver sugar out bit by bit. There could be no doubt about it.

That had left Anne scrambling to refine more sugar and make her candy at the same time.

As Anne wouldn't have enough silver sugar left after making her entry for the candy fair, it meant she didn't have the three barrels that were required.

Jonas had brought the missing silver sugar into Anne's wagon under the guise of bringing her an empty barrel. Doing so, he could steal the candy along with the wagon the moment it was finished.

Lastly, Jonas executed the final part of his plan.

He made Cathy lure the wolves to keep Challe occupied.

So he could take Anne's wagon and run off.

Jonas had successfully gotten away with one work of candy art and three barrels' worth of silver sugar.

It was half a day's ride to Lewiston.

In the afternoon, Jonas would be able to run straight there without an escort.

Anne was left with five barrels full of silver sugar, a brand-new wagon, and a worn-out old horse.

She had plenty of silver sugar. But the fair was in two days.

Actually, since it was already evening, there was really only one night and one day left.

Anne didn't have enough time to make another large sugar-candy sculpture suitable for a festival.

I can't make it in time.

The Royal Candy Fair was held every year. Even if Anne didn't make it this year, there would always be the next.

But this year's Pure Soul Day was Anne's only chance to see Emma's soul off on its way to heaven.

The sugar candy for Emma's ceremony didn't really have to be something that Anne made herself. She could get a more veteran Silver Sugar Master to create a magnificent piece of candy, and that would probably be just fine.

However, Anne wanted to send her beloved mother off with a piece of candy made by her daughter, who had achieved the title Silver Sugar Master.

This thought had been keeping Anne afloat since her mother's passing, spurring her to continue forward.

Without her motivation, Anne's willpower drained completely from her body.

Jonas's unexpected betrayal left her in shock. She had believed him to be a good person and ended up suspecting Mithril Lid Pod of eating her silver sugar. She felt foolish for her inability to believe the fairy. Just recalling Mithril's tearful eyes pained her.

Anne felt like a naive idiot for believing Jonas. She was remorseful and angry.

Those emotions filled the gap her heart, making her whole body feel sluggish and heavy.

She couldn't take a single step.

The wound on the back of her right hand, where Jonas had hit her with the whip, throbbed painfully, as if to remind her of her own foolishness.

"If I won't make it in time for this year's candy fair, there's no point," Anne muttered, placing both hands on the workbench. She hung her head and chuckled slightly.

"I'm so stupid. There I was, eagerly making my candy..."

She staggered out of the cargo hold, and the cold rain fell on her.

Anne had been drenched in a bloody liquid, and both her body and her dress were sticky and carried a terrible odor.

She was unbearably miserable.

Suddenly, she sensed someone looking at her. She saw Challe, standing beneath a tree near the wall of the way station. He had his arms folded and was looking at her with his usual arrogance.

In the end, I'm just a naive little fifteen-year-old girl.

I'm weak, I know nothing, and I have no one to depend on. I'm all alone.

Anne felt ashamed to have Challe see her in such a wretched state. She couldn't stand it. She didn't want him to look at her.

She reeled in the leather cord hanging from her neck and pulled up the little bag.

She then stalked over to Challe and thrust the bag toward him.

"I'm returning your wing."

Challe didn't move. He stared intently at the bag and asked, "We're not in Lewiston yet. Aren't you going to chase Jonas down? Aren't you going to get your candy back?"

"Jonas has already arrived in Lewiston by now. He's probably already registered for the candy fair and handed the candy sculpture over to the officials. Even if I went there now and claimed that I made the sculpture, I have no proof. They wouldn't listen to me."

"And you're okay with that?"

"Of course I'm not…but…there's nothing I can do! Even with your help… So I may as well give you your freedom. Go wherever you like!" Anne vented, hanging her head.

After a short time, Challe gently lifted the bag out of Anne's palm.

"So now we're equals?"

Anne shook her head.

"You've been my equal from the start, Challe…from start to finish. Even though that was the whole purpose of buying you, I never managed to become your master."

"Somehow, I knew that when I first saw you in the fairy market."

Challe's words were gentle. His voice was calm like the sound of the rain.

"That was why I told you to buy me. I thought that with a naive little girl, I could easily steal my wing back and escape."

"You must be happy. Everything went according to plan."

"…I'm not sure. I don't know."

Anne sensed Challe move away from the tree trunk.

He walked straight past her, slowly heading toward the iron doors of the way station.

All alone. All alone.

Something kept repeating in her head. Sobs started to escape from her throat.

All the feelings she had been bottling up came flooding out. She couldn't stop it. Everything that had been propping up Anne's heart crumbled all at once.

"Mama! Mama! Why did you die?! Why did you leave me alone? You left me alone. Why…why?!"

Anne sank to the ground. She buried her head in her knees and let the rain soak her.

How long has it been since I held my wing in my own hands?

Seven years…

No, I feel like it's been longer.

He looked down at the small leather pouch in his hand.

As the raindrops hit him, Challe Fenn Challe took in the tranquil atmosphere of a wilderness unspoiled by human hands. The way station behind him got farther away with every step.

Farther away. The girl with the sweet scent got farther away.

It was strange. Though Challe had obtained his freedom, he didn't feel happy about it.

He pondered why that was and soon understood the reason.

It was because he had never listened to any of Anne's orders. Because from the moment that Anne had purchased him, without even realizing it, he'd already achieved his freedom. So really, he had no reason to celebrate.

All that had happened was his wing had changed hands.

The one difference now was that the burden called "Anne" was no longer with him. The sweet girl who had done nothing but safely carry his wing on her breast.

He was free to choose where to go.

He was free to choose what to do.

Now that he had complete freedom, he suddenly questioned himself.

I got my freedom. So what do I want to do? Where do I want to go?

Darkness was closing in.

Break down… Something suddenly whispered in his ear.

I won't break down. If anyone's breaking down, it's her. The goal she was desperately chasing was torn away right before her eyes.

Feeling lonely? The thing whispered again, coaxing him.

Lonely?

Challe had nothing he had to protect and nowhere he had to go.

Even though this was the moment he had imagined in his dreams, the moment he regained his freedom, Challe had the feeling of receding into his own mind, of shrinking, of being isolated from the world.

Then, he felt an overwhelming longing for something.

Was it for a long-vanished memory of the distant past that would never return?

No.

Memories of the past were vacant, empty. They only chilled Challe's heart.

The thing he longed for was something warmer. Something he'd experienced more concretely.

I felt it until just a short while ago. It was…

A sweet smell. The warmth of life.

That sweet scent must have dissolved in the cold rain and vanished completely.

Challe remembered all the silver sugar that had spilled onto the ground earlier, and he stopped walking. He found himself wishing he could scoop up the scattered sugar with both hands.

As the rain continued falling on Anne, she soon became chilled from head to toe. She had already run out of tears.

Even as morning dawned and the rain lifted, she could not so much as lift her head, and she remained in a stupor.

But when she felt the brightness and warmth of the morning sun on her back, her mind suddenly cleared.

Looking up, she spotted a cluster of small blue fruits at the tip of a withered stalk of grass.

Bathed in rain and the light of the morning sun, the berries were glossy and shiny.

The color and sheen penetrated Anne's mind, which was drained of all thought.

She gazed at the cluster mindlessly.

As she did, beads of light emanated from the bunch of fruit, covering the surface of the small blue berries. It was reminiscent of the effect that appeared when Challe produced his sword. The illumination gathered on one particular berry and gradually solidified, growing to about the size of a thumb. It condensed and started to take shape.

Anne stared in awe.

The beads of light formed a small head, as well as two arms and two legs. It may have been as big as a thumb, but it was definitely taking the shape of a person. Two translucent wings unfurled on its back.

Enveloped in a veil of light was a dainty feminine figure. It was a fairy.

"...So pretty...," Anne mumbled unconsciously.

Atop the blue fruit, the fairy sat quietly with her legs folded. She vacantly surveyed her surroundings, then stretched and yawned.

The moment of a fairy's birth. Anne was enchanted by the sublime and quiet brilliance of it.

She could hardly believe that such a pure radiance existed in the world.

"Fairies are born when the energy of something condenses and takes form."

Suddenly, Anne heard a voice from behind her. She turned around in surprise.

"Challe...? Why...?"

The warrior fairy knelt down beside her.

Anne stared at him, overcome with surprise.

Without answering her question, Challe kept his eyes on the newborn and said, "Humans divide fairies into categories based on the purpose for which they use us. Worker fairies, pet fairies, warrior fairies. But we categorize ourselves based on our origin. Mithril is a water sprite. I am a stone sprite. That fairy was born from a berry, so she is a plant sprite. Her life span is probably only a year. She's short-lived. Even so, I envy her... My life span is...too long."

Fairies do not change from the time they are born until they die. Challe must have borne his current form the moment he was birthed. And fairies live about as long as the thing from which they emerge.

Challe had been born from a piece of obsidian.

Anne wondered just how long he would exist as he did now.

Trying to imagine it was mind-boggling. At the same time, she felt a

pain like she was being wrung out to dry when she heard Challe say he was jealous of the new fairy's fleeting existence.

What agony, she thought, to live alone for almost eternity.

The berry fairy seemed to have finally become conscious. She blinked her eyes rapidly and tilted her head to the side.

"Ah…a friend. And you there, you're a human, right? I seem to have just been born. I'm not even wearing a dress. Sorry about my appearance. Anyway, nice to meet you. I am Lusul El Min. Oh, I wonder why that is? I already know my own name."

The teeny-tiny fairy sounded surprised at herself. She beat her wings and flew into the air.

"You know everything that the berry from which you were birthed knows, that's all," Challe explained. "The echo of the energy that surrounds the berry turned into a sound and became your name."

"Is that so? Anyway, I would very much like a dress. Like the one that girl is wearing."

Challe gently extended his hand and let the little fairy step onto his palm.

"Lusul El Min, do not desire a dress. Wishing for such things brings you closer to humans."

"So what?"

"Humans are dangerous. They capture fairies and put them to work. They steal freedom from us."

"Really? But what about that girl? She's a human."

"That one is special. Now go, Lusul El Min. Go deeper into the wilderness. Go somewhere human hands cannot reach you and live as you please."

"How kind you are. Thank you."

The fairy thanked him, then hastily beat her wings and flew off.

After watching the little fairy go, Challe finally turned his gaze on Anne.

She was simply astonished and couldn't pull her eyes away from Challe's face. The stone sprite scowled.

"What is it? You're making a weird face."

"Am I? What are you doing here anyway? I gave your wing back, right?"

"You didn't keep your promise. I came back to make sure you do."

"My promise?"

"You promised to give me sugar candy."

"Sugar candy…?"

Did he say he came back for candy?

All alone. All alone.

The echo reverberating in Anne's head started to fade.

That can't be right. No one would bother coming back just for one piece of candy.

"So will you make it or not?" Challe asked sullenly.

Anne looked at him with a bitter smile.

Or maybe Challe really did want some candy? But either way is fine.

For this moment, at least, I'm not alone. Someone is here with me.

That made Anne happy, and a smile passed over her lips.

Her modest hopes to become a Silver Sugar Master that year and send Emma off to heaven were dashed, leaving a gaping hole in her heart.

But Challe had come back to her. Not out of obligation or under orders. He had returned on his own.

If there was something she could do for him, she might be able to prove her worth.

A single small light shone in her hollow heart.

She was happy, more than anything. Her tears threatened to spill over, but she held them back and smiled.

"That's right. I did promise, didn't I? I promised to make you something exceptionally beautiful."

Anne stood up. As far as silver sugar went, there was plenty in the wagon that Jonas had left behind.

"Wait. You can't make candy like that."

As he spoke, Challe tossed a dry cloth and a set of men's clothes over Anne's head.

She took them and tilted her head.

"Where'd you get these?"

"They were in the wagon. He left them behind. I doubt he'll mind if you use them."

Anne smiled bitterly.

"You're right."

Anne changed clothes behind the wagon.

The men's pants and shirt were baggy on her, and she folded the sleeves and hem up several times.

"My hands are too cold. I wonder if they'll even work."

Anne was freezing. She rubbed her chilly body and flexed her stiff fingers as she headed into the wagon.

Challe calmly approached her. He clasped her cold hands in his and warmed them with his breath.

"Challe…?"

She shivered at the warmth of his breath.

"Once I give you your candy, are you going to leave again?" Anne asked, unable to help herself.

As soon as she did, a soft, pleasant warmth enveloped her.

She realized that she was being gently hugged.

"You smell sweet." Challe's breath grazed her ear. "It was your fragrance that called me back. Make the candy. It's something you can do."

Anne's heart was beating fast.

When Challe let her go, she practically ran into the cargo hold.

I don't know why, but my ears are really hot.

An intense feeling of delight had welled up from the depths of her heart.

Even if Challe did leave once she handed over the candy, he had come back like this to encourage her. That alone was plenty to be happy about.

For his sake, she would make an exceptionally beautiful piece of candy.

She scooped up some silver sugar and added cold water.

She didn't even stop to think about what to make. As she kneaded the silver sugar, trying to calm the throbbing in her chest, her fingers moved on their own.

The desire to create flowed from her heart.

The image that appeared in her mind was the moment of the fairy's birth that she had just witnessed. She wanted to capture the beauty of it in silver sugar. It wouldn't have to be big. It could be small enough to sit in the palm of her hand, delicate and fragile. The thin wings and glossy, shining berries. The fairy's soft hair and dainty limbs.

Before she knew it, Anne was working the silver sugar with intense concentration.

She stretched it thinner and thinner until it was see-through, and added fretwork to the transparent membrane of sugar.

She then turned her attention to re-creating the glossy berries.

By the time Anne had finally finished her work, the light streaming into the wagon had turned a deep, brilliant orange. The sun was setting.

She was surprised at herself for having worked straight through morning and into the evening. She was also surprised by what she had created: a very small piece of candy that rested in the palm of her hand.

Anne was amazed at just how much time such a small creation had taken.

However, it was the spitting image of the fairy Anne had witnessed being birthed from the berries that morning.

Her eyes were drawn to it, and she couldn't look away. It had a certain allure.

Anne was startled to realize the similarity it bore to some of the candies Emma had made.

The candy sculpture that Anne created for the Royal Candy Fair had been impressive and a fine showpiece. But it had been one of her mother's designs. Emma had fashioned it after finding something beautiful to inspire her.

It had conveyed none of Anne's feelings.

In a way, the candy Anne had made using Emma's designs wasn't really Anne's at all.

That's why it was just an imitation…

Something she found truly beautiful and desired to capture in sugar. Using that as her inspiration, she had created a compelling, captivating piece of candy for the first time.

In that respect, Anne was certain this new piece was her best work to date.

"This is no imitation… This is my candy."

She was filled with gratitude toward Challe for accompanying her so far and decided to give the piece to him.

Holding the sugar candy carefully in both hands, Anne stepped down out of the wagon.

Challe was sitting on a rock, gazing vacantly at the setting sun, but he turned when he sensed Anne's presence.

"Challe. Here. As promised, sugar candy. It's the best I've ever made. Though it is very small compared with the one Jonas stole… Still, that one was half Mama's creation anyway. This is truly my own work."

Anne knelt in front of him and held out the candy.

Challe regarded her delicate creation and said, "…It's lovely."

Anne's cheeks flushed at his words.

She felt very happy, even happier than if he'd praised her looks. She was so delighted, she thought she might cry.

"Thank you. Will you accept it?"

Challe carefully claimed the sugar candy with both hands.

Now he's probably going to go off somewhere.

With that thought, the fairy before Anne seemed like the loveliest being in the world.

His beautiful wing reflected the sunset, and she wanted to knows its texture before he left.

"Your wing. Would you let me touch it?"

Anne didn't think that Challe would let her casually handle something that held his very life force. He would be making himself vulnerable, giving her the opportunity to damage him if she wanted to cause harm.

She knew all that but couldn't help but ask.

But Challe nodded.

"Touch it."

"You're sure?"

After waiting for him to nod again, Anne gently scooped up Challe's wing in both hands.

The wing was faintly warm. She let it slip through her hands. It had a texture that sent a shiver down her spine, smoother than silk. Then, she lightly kissed it.

Challe shuddered suddenly, raised his chin slightly, and narrowed his eyes. He exhaled sharply.

Anne released his wing and smiled.

"Thank you."

"Are you satisfied?"

"Yes. So now…"

Now you can go, she tried to say, but the words were stuck in her throat.

She actually didn't want him to go anywhere.

For some time, Challe gazed down at the candy in his hand. He then asked curtly, "This sugar candy is mine, right?"

"Mm-hmm."

"So you'll let me do anything I want with it?"

As he said this, Challe rose. He untied the rope from the tree that secured Anne's horse and hitched it to the remaining wagon.

He then walked back over to Anne, whose head was tilted in puzzlement. Challe jerked his chin toward the carriage.

"Get in the driver's seat. We're heading out."

"Where to?"

"Lewiston. If we ride through the night, we'll arrive in Lewiston by morning. We should make it just in time for the day of the Royal Candy Fair. You want to become a Silver Sugar Master this year, don't you?"

"But, Challe, my entry—"

"We've got this."

Challe held the candy in his palms out to Anne.

Prompted by his expression, Anne once again took her own work of candy art into her hands.

"If that really is your best work, then we should submit it. If it doesn't win, then you can give up."

All the entries for the Royal Candy Fair were always large and ostentatious. It was likely that a small piece like Anne's would go completely unnoticed among them. It would probably be rejected.

But Anne had finally realized something.

She wondered why she had been in such a hurry to become a Silver Sugar Master. She obviously wasn't ready, and even if she had somehow managed it by mimicking her mother's brilliance, it wouldn't have made Emma happy. Her mother would never have a peaceful journey to heaven with a piece of candy made by a fake Silver Sugar Master.

If the small sculpture really showed Anne's true ability, then she ought to compete with it. She looked up at Challe.

"Why are you doing this for me? I gave you your wing back."

"Indeed, I have my wing back, and you are not my master. So we can become friends—if you want."

"Do you want that, Challe?"

The warrior fairy shrugged.

"Maybe."

Anne could sense some hidden meaning behind his curt reply.

The natural brilliance returned to Anne's eyes. Happiness imbued her with a surge of strength.

"It'll be night soon. Do you think we can make it down the Bloody Highway safely? Will we be okay?"

Challe smiled boldly.

"Who do you take me for?"

They dashed through the night. Anne's horse did very well, and though its breath became haggard, it never faltered. They exited the Bloody Highway at dawn.

Before the morning dew had even dried, the royal capital of Lewiston spread out before their eyes.

Chapter 7
WHAT BECAME OF THE ROYAL MEDAL

Atop a small hill surrounded by a moat stood an enormous, sprawling castle. Eight large, cobblestone boulevards radiated out from the hill with the castle at its center, as if to draw all eyes to the monarch inside.

The Royal Candy Fair was held on the broadest of the eight thoroughfares, the triumphal road that led directly to the front gate of the castle. A white tent had been erected in the plaza before the castle gate, and underneath it was a riser with seats meant for the members of the royal family attending the fair.

Such festivals were very popular in the royal capital. The plaza was crowded with people trying to get a glimpse of the royal family.

Sitting at the center of everyone's attention were the king and queen. With them were the princesses and princes. Anyone would sigh at their dazzling outfits and gorgeous looks.

In front of the royal seating stood a long table covered with a white sheet. On top of the table sat a line of sugar-candy sculptures, each so large that a person could have barely wrapped their arms around them.

Every single one of them was sure to be richly colored with detailed handiwork.

But at the moment, all the candy sculptures were covered with cloth, obscuring what lay beneath.

Behind each of the entries stood the crafter who had made it. Since they were appearing before the king, all were dressed in their finest clothes.

Jonas was there, too, wearing a splendid fur vest.

The man in charge of the Royal Candy Fair was the Earl of Downing. He was an old man who had distinguished himself for his tact as the minister of home affairs during the previous king's reign. He had since withdrawn from that position, but even so, he was an elder statesman greatly trusted by the current monarch.

This esteemed gentleman confirmed that all the candy artists in attendance and that every member of the royal family was seated.

Just as the Earl of Downing was standing to make the opening announcement that would begin the judging process—

—a section of the crowd began to stir.

The earl scowled, wondering what could possibly be the matter, as a single boxy wagon came charging through the spectators.

"Watch out!!"

"Stop that wagon!"

The guards ran forward, and the small girl driving the carriage yanked on the reins and pulled her horse to a stop. She then jumped down from the driver's seat, slipped right past all the guards, and rushed into the plaza.

Behind her, as if to protect her, was a young man with black hair.

The girl was trying to dash to the front of the tent where the Earl of Downing stood.

"Seize her!"

One of the guards grabbed the girl's arm, but her raven-haired protector unleashed a hard kick to the man's stomach. The guard was sent sprawling into the crowd. The girl was free again.

The young man shouted to the girl, "Go!"

She kept running.

The bold fellow fearlessly fought against the guards and their spears, preventing any of them from following.

That was when people finally noticed that the young man had a single beautiful wing on his back.

"Don't you touch that girl!"

"Are you…a fairy?!"

Right in front of the tent where the Earl of Downing still stood, the intruder, who had been running at full speed, tripped. She lost her footing and pitched forward.

But even after tumbling to the ground, she kept her face up and shouted desperately, out of breath:

"I can see you haven't yet announced the opening of the Royal Candy Fair. If that's the case, then it should still be possible for me to enter, which I would like to do. I am a candy crafter. My name is Anne Halford. My place of origin is unknown!"

A guard leaped from the tent and pinned Anne where she had fallen. "You disrespectful wretch!" he shouted.

However, a cheerful, amused voice interjected from behind the stunned earl. "Just when I thought you weren't coming! My, my, what a flashy entrance that was!! You truly are an interesting specimen, Anne."

Anne's eyes went wide at the sound of the familiar voice.

A young aristocrat stepped out from behind the earl. He wore formal clothing ornamented with silver embroidery. Without a doubt, it was the attire of the Silver Sugar Viscount.

The man wearing it had a familiar face and wild brown eyes.

"Hugh?!"

"Mercury. Do you know this girl?" the Earl of Downing asked Hugh.

Mercury?

Anne focused on the familiar man's face.

Hugh Mercury?! The maestro of the Mercury Workshop and the current Silver Sugar Viscount?!

"Yes. I know for a fact that this girl is a simple candy crafter. There's no need to be alarmed. The fairy over there is her bodyguard."

Hearing this, the Earl of Downing raised his hand and gestured toward the guards, who were still holding their spears at the ready.

"Fine. Stand down over there. This girl wishes to enter the competition."

The guards surrounding Challe and the one pinning Anne down all followed the earl's orders and stepped back.

Anne pushed herself to her knees.

The Earl of Downing looked back at her and asked, "I can see that you are young. Despite your youth, you announce your intention to enter. You seem to know what you are doing. Who taught you?"

"My mother. My mother was a Silver Sugar Master."

"I see. Your statement of entry was well-made. But are you aware that there are other procedures?"

"Yes. The candy crafter states their intention to enter to the Earl of Downing, then after that, the Silver Sugar Viscount will ascertain whether the crafter is skilled enough that their work will not offend the eyes of His Majesty the King by making them produce a simple piece of candy. Once deemed acceptable, the candidate will be permitted to enter."

"That's right. And that process finished yesterday. Furthermore, His Majesty is already in attendance, and we are about to start the candy fair. There is no time to test your skill now."

"I will complete the test as quickly as possible. Please let me try!"

The Earl of Downing seemed moved by her desperation and turned back to Hugh to consult with him.

"What do you say, Mercury?"

"There is no time to test her now."

His response was curt. Anne bit her lip and cast her eyes down.

But Hugh kept grinning.

"However, Earl, as luck would have it, I tested this girl's skills just the other day. I know that they will not offend the eyes of His Majesty."

At those words, Anne lifted her head. When her eyes met Hugh's, he gave her a cheerful wink.

The Earl of Downing nodded.

"Very well. If the Silver Sugar Viscount deems you worthy, you are permitted to enter."

He pointed to the table where the candy sculptures were all lined up.

"Now then, go and get your three barrels of silver sugar and give them to the guards so they can carry them to the edge of the plaza. Then, set the candy you have made over there, stand behind it, and await the judgment of the royal family."

"Yes, sir. Thank you very much."

Anne stood up and bowed in gratitude. She dusted off her now dirt-covered clothes.

The curious gazes of the onlookers and the participating candy crafters followed Anne as she stepped out into the middle of the plaza.

Her competitors were all dressed in their finest.

Anne, on the other hand, wore baggy men's clothes that didn't fit her, and her hair and face were dirty. Her slim body looked even skinnier than it was, and she looked much younger than her age. She also had a beautiful fairy accompanying her, the likes of whom no one had ever seen before.

Who could that be? People whispered to one another as they stared in curiosity.

Oddly enough, the spot where Anne had been told to line up was right next to Jonas.

Jonas had nervously watched everything unfold.

When Anne stood beside him, he sneered and tried to act tough.

"Wow, Anne, my clothes look great on you, don't they? Anyway, you have a candy sculpture?"

Anne shot Jonas an intense glare.

"Thanks for your concern. These clothes came in handy. And don't worry about me; I've got my candy."

"Well then, hurry up and put it on the table. Where is it?"

"Right here."

Anne stepped forward and set a small object covered in a cloth atop the white table.

Scornful laughter erupted among the spectators and candy crafters when they saw it.

Jonas snorted with laughter as well.

"Well, considering the time, I suppose that's about the best you could do, huh? I'm impressed by your courage, Anne. To think you would enter with a piece the size of a child's treat."

Staring at the royal family's tent directly in front of her, Anne answered, "I'm astonished by you, too, Jonas. Entering someone else's work—how shameless can you be?"

"I've got no idea what you're talking about."

"Do you think you can fool Hugh's eye? He's the Silver Sugar Viscount. You ought to know how attentive he is from what happened at the Doctor's Inn."

Jonas's expression stiffened ever so slightly, but his mouth immediately relaxed into a smile.

"When I registered, I was surprised to learn that Hugh was the Silver Sugar Viscount. But he only became Viscount six months ago. He acts self-important, but he's new to the post. He didn't say a thing when he saw *my candy* that I brought this time."

"There's no way he doesn't know."

"I wonder?"

After making sure that Anne's piece had been placed on the table, the Earl of Downing raised his hand and made the announcement.

"The Royal Candy Fair is hereby open. The title of Silver Sugar Master shall be granted to the most outstanding candy crafter in the kingdom."

One of the officials managing the candy fair instructed the crafters, "Everyone, present your sugar candy to His Majesty."

When he said this, they all simultaneously removed the cloths covering their sculptures.

The onlookers sighed when they saw the row of gorgeous candies.

The king was leaning on his armrest, sweeping a cursory gaze over the entries from right to left, not showing much interest.

Then, the king's eyes stopped. He leaned forward.

His focus was directed toward Jonas and Anne.

No way, did I catch his attention?!

Anne's heartbeat quickened.

The king beckoned the Earl of Downing over and whispered something into his ear.

The earl nodded and walked over to the pair.

"You two crafters. Jonas Anders and Anne Halford. Bring your candies to His Majesty."

Jonas and Anne locked eyes.

The spectators were puzzled and whispered to one another.

"The one on that side is clearly impressive. It surpasses all the rest; it's an easy win. So why are they summoning that little one up in front of the king?"

"Don't know; I can hardly see it from here."

With the aid of a guard, Jonas set his sculpture on a table before the king. He knelt, his face stiff with nerves.

Anne nodded to Challe, who was standing in the crowd.

"Here I go."

Cradling her candy gently in her hands, she carried it up to the king. She placed it on the table and knelt as well.

The king serenely rose to his feet and studied the sugar candies.

"How curious. Come here and take a look, Mercury."

In a quiet voice, he called over the Silver Sugar Viscount.

Hugh approached the king's side and nodded.

"The character of the pieces is similar, isn't it? As if both candies were created by the same artist."

At his words, Jonas cringed. Hugh's eyes brightened.

"Your Majesty, which do you prefer?"

The king narrowed his scrutiny at Hugh's question. His gaze was fixed on the small fairy sculpture.

"I like this one. It looks like it might shatter at any moment. It's ephemeral. Yet it's also truly alive. I've never seen such a beautiful piece of candy."

"Indeed."

"I think that this sugar candy is the best. How about it? I am of the opinion that this candy crafter is worthy of becoming a Silver Sugar Master."

No way, no way, Anne thought, her heart pounding faster as she continued staring at the ground.

However—

"That candy sculpture is truly splendid, Your Majesty, but…"

—from behind the king came the queen's calm voice.

"But, Your Majesty, the requirement was to make something large and flashy to serve as a centerpiece for the festival. Even if she has the skill to make this small piece, it remains a question whether she has the ability to create something sizable. I think you ought to consider what qualities make someone worthy of the title."

"That is true…"

The king was silent for a while. Anne's heartbeat quickened even more.

"I've decided," the king pronounced. "I have decided. This crafter is worthy of becoming a Silver Sugar Master. Your name?"

The Earl of Downing answered:

"Jonas Anders."

"All right, then, I will make the proclamation. I award the royal medal to the sugar candy brought forth by Jonas Anders. The person who made this work is this year's Silver Sugar Master."

The spectators stirred.

When she sensed Jonas lift his head, Anne went limp.

Of course.

"Now, Anne Halford, please step back. Jonas Anders, remain up here. The guards will bring the three barrels of silver sugar you refined up to me. You will show them to His Majesty and then present it and your candy sculpture to the kingdom."

"Yes, sir."

Jonas's cheeks flushed with excitement, and he threw out his chest proudly.

After glancing briefly at his face, Anne bowed to the members of the royal family once more and picked up her candy.

Jonas's three barrels of silver sugar were carried before the king.

Anne had just turned her back on them when she heard—

"Wh-what?! What is this?!"

Jonas shouted in a loud voice that was inappropriate in the presence of the king.

Anne wheeled back around to look.

Something flew energetically out of one of the barrels that had been placed before Jonas. As they watched it flit away nimbly, Jonas, the king, and the Earl of Downing were all speechless.

A small fairy had emerged from the barrel. A fairy with silver hair and blue eyes. It was Mithril Lid Pod.

Anne gasped.

"What is the meaning of this, Anders?!" the earl bellowed after recovering from his shock and peering into the container from which Mithril had exited. "One whole barrel of silver sugar is completely empty!"

"Th-that can't be!"

Jonas was flabbergasted as Mithril prostrated himself before the king in Jonas's place.

"Aaaaaah!! Please forgive me, Your Royal Highness, sir! I am but a lowly worker fairy employed by my master, Jonas Anders. My master is extremely unskilled at refining silver sugar, and although he managed to create a fine candy sculpture, he was not able prepare the amount of silver sugar required. He ordered me to employ my skills of deception and make it appear as if there was silver sugar filling this barrel, then he shut me in. But I think it's terrible to deceive you, Your Royal Highness, sir, and I just couldn't do it!!"

Mithril flailed dramatically in a performance worthy of any stage. He even pulled out a tiny handkerchief that he'd somehow thought to have on hand, biting down on it as he wailed.

Anne was stunned.

Why is Mithril here? What is he doing?!

Then, she noticed something.

As Mithril stood there bawling, Anne saw that his stomach was bulging, stretched almost to bursting.

Is it possible Mithril ate that whole barrel of silver sugar…?

Anne didn't know how the little fairy had ended up inside one of the barrels that Jonas had hauled to the fair.

But she could only think of one reason for him to put on such a display.

He was doing it for her.

This was his attempt to repay Anne after her candy had been stolen.

"This is all a plot!!" Jonas leaped and protested loudly, seemingly having forgotten that he was in the presence of the king. "This worker fairy is under the command of that crafter right there! He belongs to Anne Halford! I expect the Silver Sugar Viscount knows this as well!! She and I are acquaintances. She's been harassing me in all sorts of ways, just 'cause she wants to become a Silver Sugar Master herself! This is another of her schemes."

Anne was stunned by his terrible false accusation. Jonas yanked her violently by the arm.

"Get over here, you coward!!"

"Ow!!"

When he saw Anne shriek, Mithril's expression changed, and he jumped into the air.

"Which one of you is the coward?! Let go of Anne, you scumbag!!"

He stopped his crying act and shouted angrily.

When he did, Jonas pointed at Mithril triumphantly.

"There, see for yourself!! This girl and her fairy have known each other from the start. We ought to kill this foolish fairy right away."

"I won't let you do that!"

At those words, Anne flared up and shook her arm free from Jonas's grip.

She turned to face the royal family's tent.

She could no longer stay quiet after Jonas mentioned killing Mithril. It was his most craven behavior so far.

"It's true, that fairy is an acquaintance of mine, and he also did this for my sake. But there is a reason for that. The candy this person, Jonas Anders, is calling his own, the piece that he submitted, is one I made. He stole my candy. He was planning to become a Silver Sugar Master with my work, and this fairy was trying to stop him."

"That's a lie! I didn't steal it!"

"You're going to keep lying even now?!"

"Shut up! You are the liar!"

Anne and Jonas glared furiously at each other.

The spectators, every member of the royal family, even the Earl of Downing—each person in the plaza was shocked and perplexed by Anne's and Jonas's claims.

Exactly which of them was lying? They all wondered.

Only Hugh wore a faint smile.

"Well then, will you allow me to clarify things, Your Majesty?" Hugh asked the king, who was staring at the two crafters with a sour look on his face.

"The question is, which one of them made this candy sculpture? The artist who created it is the rightful Silver Sugar Master. In that case, allow me to ascertain who it was."

"Indeed. Do you have a method for determining that, Mercury? If so, you may do so."

"Yes, sir. Now then—"

Hugh whispered some orders to a man standing off to the side who appeared to be his valet. Once the valet had left the royal family's tent, Hugh stood in front of Anne and Jonas.

"I'll have you do the same thing you did at the Doctor's Inn that night. But this time, there's a theme."

Another small table was carried in and set before the king. On top of the table, two types of basins containing cold water and all the tools needed to make sugar candy—spatulas and rulers, various sizes of cotton swabs and the like—were quickly arranged.

"This is the work that His Majesty selected. The sculpture includes some small butterflies, here and here. You will make identical ones now, in front of His Majesty's own eyes. That way, we will be able to see, by examining your butterflies, just whose hand crafted this candy."

"Understood. I'm ready."

Anne nodded. It was exactly what she'd hoped for.

But Jonas looked pale.

"All good, Jonas?"

Jonas managed to nod when prompted.

Anne and Jonas stood beside each other at the table.

Anne could feel the curious stares of the onlookers all around them, and the members of the royal family watched them coldly.

With the silver sugar right in front of her, she closed her eyes softly.

She could feel a kind pair of eyes gazing at her. Somehow, she knew they belonged to Challe.

Make a butterfly. An exceptionally beautiful butterfly, one that would make Challe happy.

"Begin!"

Anne opened her eyes at the sound of Hugh's voice. She added cold water to her silver sugar.

She kneaded it and brought out the luster of the sugar dough.

Let's knead it more. I want the wings to be glossy. Yeah, I want to make beautiful wings like Challe's.

Once the silver sugar was in her hands, strangely enough, Anne ceased to care about Jonas, who was banging around, making clumsy noises beside her.

Sweat was beading on Jonas's forehead. From time to time, he clicked his tongue.

Anne's fingers moved nimbly.

More beautiful.

Challe was watching. That gave Anne great peace of mind. Due to his presence, she was free from any doubt.

"That's enough."

The sound of Hugh's voice startled Anne.

When she looked up, Hugh was standing right in front of her. She hadn't noticed him approaching. Next to him was the king, having emerged from his tent once again.

His Majesty had been intently observing the two crafters at work.

Jonas's hands were shaking, and he had sunk to the ground where he stood.

"Anders's butterfly isn't even worth considering," Hugh said.

The sugar-candy butterfly Jonas had been working on had only barely taken the shape of a butterfly at all.

It certainly didn't seem like it would be anyone's top choice. It was clearly inferior to the sculpture that had been chosen by the king.

Hugh looked at Anne's workspace next.

"Halford's butterfly… It resembles the butterflies on the candy that Your Majesty chose, but it is different."

Anne looked down at her own hands.

There was a beautiful butterfly there.

It was much more modest than the ones decorating the candy sculpture the king had selected, yet it had a charm to it, like it might start fluttering its wings at any moment. It was a pure-white butterfly, devoid of color, but the way it reflected the light made it look rainbow-hued.

The king scowled.

"What's the meaning of this, Mercury?"

Hugh shrugged and smiled. "I don't know. Ultimately, I'm not sure which of them made the candy sculpture that you selected, Your Majesty."

The king looked back and forth between the butterflies the pair had made.

"But it seems obvious to me which of these crafters made the work that I selected…"

"Well then, take a look at Halford's butterfly and the butterflies on the winning sculpture, Your Majesty. Which do you like better?"

"Halford's butterfly, of course. Compared with those on the sculpture, it's more…" The king looked surprised, like he had just realized something. He then smiled. "I see. They're not the same; is that what you mean?"

"Yes. So I cannot say for certain which of these two made the sculpture."

Jonas jumped on those words, as if he had discovered one last chance to escape.

"I—I can't make anything unless I work quietly, alone!! So if you allow me to take my time and work by myself somewhere quiet, I'll be able to recreate the same butterflies that are on the piece His Majesty so kindly selected. Really. I swear to you, it's true."

If it was proven that Jonas had taken credit for someone else's work, he would be guilty of attempting to deceive the king. That was a capital offense, and he might even be beheaded.

"Your conduct is unseemly, Jonas," said Hugh.

Jonas's protests grew even louder.

"But I'm not lying!! You have no proof that I'm lying!!"

"You say you're not lying?" the king asked solemnly.

The plaza fell silent for a moment at the dignified sound of the king's voice.

Trembling, Jonas prostrated himself.

"I swear to god, I am not telling you a lie."

Next, the king looked at Anne.

"And you're not lying, are you, Halford?"

"No."

Without hesitation, Anne met His Majesty's gaze. When she did, the king grinned.

"If neither of you is lying, then I really don't know what to do. And without any evidence, I can't make a proper judgment. I can't bestow glory on either of you. Downing!!"

"Sir."

The elderly retainer approached the king's side when summoned.

"It appears there is no one here qualified to become a Silver Sugar Master this year. The contest is over!"

The king turned on his heel. Casting a backward glance at the bewildered royal family and their assorted retainers, he calmly departed the tent.

The spectators looked at one another.

"What's going on?"

"There's no royal medal?"

"They're not going to pick another sculpture?"

"I mean, the king already left…"

"It doesn't look like they're going to pick one."

The king had selected a sculpture and then taken his leave.

But it was still unclear who had actually made the piece.

It was an unprecedented turn of events.

In the end, no one was named Silver Sugar Master at that year's Royal Candy Fair.

The queen rose to her feet. She was astounded by her husband's actions. Sparing a quick glance at the dumbfounded Anne, she summoned the earl, whispered something to him, and departed as well.

There was commotion among the candy crafters, who exchanged various looks amongst themselves. Once it was clear, though, that the king was not going to resume the candy fair, they gave up and started making arrangements to leave.

The spectators also milled about, chatting noisily.

The Earl of Downing walked slowly to Anne's side.

"Anne Halford. I have a message from the queen."

Anne turned to him in surprise, and the elder statesman informed her quietly, "Her Majesty says that next year, you are to bring a sugar-candy sculpture worthy of a celebration. She looks forward to seeing your work."

The moment she understood the meaning behind the queen's words, Anne's heart filled with joy. Her cheeks flushed red.

"Yes… Yes! Definitely. I'll definitely be here!"

"By the way, Halford. If you don't already have a buyer for that fairy sculpture, would you sell it to me? My granddaughter is planning to get married soon, and I've been looking for a splendid candy sculpture for the occasion. How does six hundred cress sound?"

Six hundred cress. That meant six gold pieces. It was a dizzying sum of money. It would buy two horses and a brand-new wagon. Anne felt faint just thinking about it. But she shook her head.

"I'm terribly sorry, Earl. I've already promised this to someone."

"It's six hundred cress."

"…I'm very sorry."

"I see. That's too bad. Well, I suppose if you weren't a bit eccentric, you wouldn't have been able to create something like that in the first place. By the way, Mercury. I'm leaving Anders's fate up to you. As Silver Sugar Viscount, take whatever measures you see fit."

"Leave it to me, Earl."

Hugh gave an exaggerated bow.

"Well then, Halford. See you again next year." With one last cordial smile, the elderly statesman turned his back to them, leaving Anne and Jonas behind in all the commotion.

Hugh looked down at them with his hands on his hips.

"Now then, Anne. It's too bad it turned out this way, but what should we do? Dealing with Jonas has been left entirely to me, after all." His tone was quite casual. "Is there anything you want to say to the boy? Anything you'd like me to do with him? I am not inclined to be as kind as His Majesty, you know. I've got no problem lopping off the head of one measly candy crafter."

Anne was startled to see Jonas slumped in the same spot. He hadn't looked up, and his body trembled.

Unnoticed by Anne, Salim had appeared behind Hugh. He was regarding Jonas with predatory eyes.

Anne shook her head.

"Hugh…Viscount, you have my gratitude. Thank you for supporting my entry."

"Come now, you don't have to be that formal. Hugh is fine."

Hugh patted her head, and Anne shrugged.

"I really am grateful, Hugh. Thank you. I've had enough of Jonas. There's nothing I want to say to him. Nothing I want to say, but…"

Jonas looked defeated, like he had already taken plenty of punishment for his foolish actions.

At this point, she had no words for him. There was, however, still something she wanted to get off her chest.

"Stand up, Jonas," she instructed him quietly, but Jonas didn't move.

"Stand up," she repeated.

Jonas stood sluggishly, keeping his face pointed toward the ground.

"Jonas!! Look at me!!"

The instant he looked up in surprise, Anne slapped his face. She watched coldly as he withdrew in shock. Then, she grinned cheerfully.

"Ah, what a relief! I wanted to give him one good smack! I'm good now."

"A fitting punishment!"

Hugh roared with laughter. Behind him, Salim let out a quiet laugh.

"Great, so that's that!!"

At Hugh's words, Anne quickly curtsied. Hugh smiled and nodded back at her. The two then took off walking in opposite directions.

Jonas was left standing in the same spot. He raised a hand to touch his cheek where Anne had slapped him.

Cathy rushed over to Jonas and gently grabbed his trouser hem.

Anne searched for a pair of black eyes in the plaza's jumbled crowd.

Challe was a short distance away, watching her.

She walked slowly toward him, her sugar candy in her hand.

"Challe. Thank you. I wasn't able to become this year's Silver Sugar Master, but I'll participate again next year. I didn't achieve my goal in time to send Mama off to heaven, but...but Mama will have to make do with the best candy I can create right now."

Anne had been fixated on becoming the Silver Sugar Master that year, but those feelings had now faded.

Because she missed her mother so much, she had been consumed with the idea of giving Emma a proper send-off to the next life. She had been desperately chasing that goal to avoid having to confront her sadness and loneliness.

Having been made aware of this, it was as if the clouds had disappeared from her heart. She felt like she was finally able to accept Emma's death.

It was all thanks to those black eyes in front of her.

Even if Challe disappeared as soon as she handed him the candy, that wouldn't erase the fact that he had returned for her sake. Somewhere in the world, even if just for a moment, someone had cared about Anne. That alone made her feel like she could keep living.

Now Anne felt like she could pursue her own dream. Her dream of becoming a Silver Sugar Master. A future she chose for herself and not for her mother's sake.

I will become a Silver Sugar Master. No matter how many years it takes...

A new purpose was born in her heart.

I will become a Silver Sugar Master and surpass Mama.

"I'm feeling motivated now, and it's all because of you, Challe. Thank you. As promised, this sugar-candy sculpture is yours, so I'm giving it back."

Anne's chest was tight with sadness over his departure. Nevertheless, she couldn't stop smiling now that she had finally latched onto a real aspiration.

Challe stared at the candy being offered to him. But he huffed and immediately turned away.

"It looks gross."

"Huh?!" Anne shouted.

"When it comes to sugar candy, beautiful craftsmanship imparts a delicious flavor. Badly made candies don't taste nice. I want an exquisite candy made by a Silver Sugar Master."

"Wh-what are you talking about? Are you saying this one isn't good enough?"

"It's not good enough."

"So how am I supposed to make something better than this?!"

Anne wondered why Challe would say something so hateful at such a moment.

The sweet emotions Anne had felt when she'd looked into Challe's beautiful eyes vanished all at once.

Then, Challe said smoothly, "I'll claim my candy on this day next year. I don't need it until then. I'll stay with you until you become a Silver Sugar Master."

Anne blinked in surprise.

"Huh...? With me?"

"Is that so bad?"

Challe seemed displeased as he cast a sharp glance at Anne.

"It's not...bad. Not at all. But...why?"

Challe looked offended and acted like he couldn't think of a good response. However, after a little while, his expression softened.

Instead of answering the question, he took Anne's right hand in his. And then—

"Anne."

—almost in a whisper, he called her name. It was the first time he had ever spoken it. Anne felt her chest grow hot.

Challe gently placed a kiss on Anne's fingers. Almost tenderly.

It was as if he was swearing some sort of vow.

Anne didn't understand the meaning behind the kiss, but her heart was pounding so hard, she could barely think.

Challe looked directly at her.

He's got beautiful eyes. Truthful and honest eyes.

Anne felt a surge of affection unlike any she had experienced before. It was somewhat different from the fondness she felt for her friends.

It was probably the feeling of first love.

Just then—

"Hey, did you see?! Did you see my performance of a lifetime?!"

—with a cheerful voice, Mithril Lid Pod came bounding across the plaza. Challe casually released Anne's hand.

With one large jump, Mithril landed softly on Anne's shoulder.

Anne was bursting with regret and delight.

"Mithril!"

Without thinking, she grabbed the little fairy and hugged him tightly.

"I'm sorry! I'm sorry, Mithril, I'm so sorry. I shouldn't have suspected you of eating my silver sugar, even for a second. I was stupid, so stupid for not trusting you. I'm sorry. Forgive me."

"I—I—I—I—I—I am Mithril Lid Pod! D-don't abbreviate it! Anyway, it's not a question of forgiving you or not. I would never act that way unless it was to help you."

Even though Mithril had flushed bright red, when he pulled himself out of Anne's arms, he rubbed his upper lip boastfully.

"But I still suspected you," Anne said, "even if it was just for a moment."

"Hmph. The thing with humans is that you're all dummies. I'd already factored in that you're a dummy, too, Anne. It was no surprise you'd make a mistake like that, and it doesn't change the fact that I was determined

to repay my debt to you. I'm a fairy, after all. If I gave up on repaying you that easily, it would hurt the reputation of fairies everywhere!"

Mithril threw out his chest proudly despite having said some very rude things.

"I saw the nasty trick that guy was playing and decided I would take him down. He's just awful, huh? I figured I would embarrass him and ate up one of his barrels of silver sugar!"

Mithril cackled with laughter, which was quickly cut short by a sickened groan.

"I ate a whole barrel of silver sugar, in fact… I think I'm gonna be sick… Uuugh."

Thinking about how fairies ate, Anne hadn't the slightest idea where or what a fairy might throw up. However, given that Mithril did look like he might expel some unimaginable substance from somewhere unspeakable, Anne took a step back out of the line of fire.

"Well, honestly, I didn't even help that much… In fact, I feel like I might have trapped you in a difficult predicament…" Mithril reflected quietly, despite his earlier boasting.

"Not at all! Thank you. But how did you know Jonas had stolen my sugar-candy sculpture? Did you follow us secretly?"

"I was inside your wagon the whole time, Anne."

"Huh?"

In her surprise, Anne turned to look at Challe, and he shrugged.

"After Mithril Lid Pod was accused of stealing the silver sugar, he took refuge in the cargo hold of your wagon to hide. He disappeared from your sight, as requested."

"I-in a sense…"

Jonas had stolen Anne's wagon, where Mithril had been hiding. Ultimately, the cunning fairy had taken him down.

Mithril Lid Pod snorted with laughter.

"Did you forget? I'm sticking with you at any cost to repay my debt, Anne. I'll follow you to the depths of hell!"

"But you just exposed Jonas and ruined his plan; surely, that's sufficient?"

"I've still got a long way to go! My debt to you is nothing so minor as that! You'll have to accept a much grander repayment!"

"Ah, ha-ha-ha…a grand repayment…?"

That could mean anything. Somehow, Anne felt frightened.

Challe muttered, "Have you ever heard the phrase *unsolicited acts of kindness*, Mithril Lid Pod?"

"Nope, sorry! And what about you? Why are you here? You made it to Lewiston, so I thought softhearted Anne was going to set you free. Aren't you at liberty to go wherever you want now? Why are you still hanging around?!"

"There's something I need to get from the scarecrow."

He called her scarecrow again.

Anne felt dejected.

I could have sworn he called me Anne just a moment ago… Could I have imagined it?

"You're a rude jerk to the very end, Challe Fenn Challe! No matter how much Anne favors you, even if she does look just like a scarecrow, you can't call her that all the time!"

"What's wrong with calling a scarecrow a scarecrow?"

"Listen, you!! Don't call her 'scarecrow, scarecrow' over and over again!"

"You're the one calling her scarecrow over and over."

"Anyway! Even if it's the truth, there are things in this world that you should and shouldn't say! Like 'scarecrow, scarecrow'!! It's too on the nose; it's not even funny!!"

Anne smiled weakly. "You guys… Can you both give it a rest with the rude comments?"

When she said that, both fairies seemed to suddenly realize what they were doing. They exchanged glances and stopped arguing.

I didn't make it as Silver Sugar Master this year. But Her Majesty told me to come back again next year. That's enough for me.

The obsidian fairy said he wanted a delicious piece of candy.

The water-droplet fairy wanted to repay a debt she didn't need repaid.

Anne knew that at least she wouldn't be alone anymore.

I am not alone. Someday, I'll probably become a Silver Sugar Master. I have a future. That's the best I could ask for.

Anne smiled.

"Well, it doesn't matter. Whether I'm a scarecrow or you're a crow, I'm going to make sugar candies for you two. Wonderful candies. That's all I can do."

The sky was high and clear overhead.

The sweet aroma of many sugar candies hung in the air over the royal plaza.

AFTERWORD

Nice to meet you, everyone. My name is Miri Mikawa.

This book is a revised edition of the work that received the Special Jury Award in the Seventh Beans Novel Contest.

When I sent in my entry, the thing I was most worried about was that I might have mistakenly violated the rules of the competition. I realize that's not what I should have been concerned about, but at that time, I was afraid the judges would toss my manuscript out without even reading it because of a transgression.

I read the application rules carefully, and the one that gave me the most trouble was the stipulation that the books had to be "between one hundred fifty and three hundred pages when converted to a four-hundred-character manuscript paper." I wondered whether the white spaces counted as characters for the conversion.

I wanted to ask someone, but I didn't know anyone who might have had the answer. Besides, even if I had known someone, I was sure it was a stupid question… A bit like asking, *Teacher, do bananas count as a snack?*

So I decided that, regardless of whether the line breaks and blank spaces were included in the character count or not, I would make sure that my page count wouldn't fall outside the range stated in the rules. That way, I would be safe.

I trimmed down the dialogue and further refined the story.

I ended up with a manuscript that met the page count.

Then when the manuscript was being turned into a book, it wound up several dozen pages too short, and I found out I needed to revise it.

I had been overly worried about the rules of the contest and had cut my work to satisfy the conditions, but it turned out to be shorter than a typical book.

But thanks to being allowed to make revisions, I had a little more leeway to expand my tightly-packed story.

I hope it's at least a little better now than what I originally submitted.

I have nothing but gratitude for the esteemed judges who carefully read through the manuscript that I so nervously submitted and selected it as a winner. I'd also like to express my heartfelt thanks to everyone in the editorial department who kindly read it after it was chosen and to everyone who was part of the selection process.

In addition, I need to thank the managers who were very friendly and considerate to someone like me, who is still so useless. I say a little prayer whenever I'm treated so nicely. Thank you so much. I look forward to working with you in the future.

And—and I have to mention Aki, who drew the illustrations. I can't tell you how happy I was when I learned that you would be drawing for me. The pictures of Anne and Challe that you illustrated are just wonderful. They're such lucky characters!

I'm getting to the end here, but now I need to say something to all the people who picked up a copy of this book.

If it wasn't to your liking, I am truly sorry. My apologies. Please have a laugh and forget all about it.

If it was to your liking, hooray! Thank you, I love you!

To each and every one of you, once again, thank you very much.

Miri Mikawa